I0648199

FOREVER LEARNING

D.L. Hatton

This is a work of fiction. All the characters and events portrayed in this book are either products of the author's imagination or are used fictitiously.

FOREVER LEARNING

Copyright 2006 by David Hatton

All rights reserved, including the right to reproduce this book, or portions thereof, in any form.

ISBN: 978-0-6151-3892-3

Preface

For many years Ross and Julia have enjoyed teaching together in the same high school but as times change, discipline falters and Ross begins to search and study the root causes of his growing dissatisfaction, a chasm begins to develop between them. Not only that but he gets into trouble with the school district. His parents, both school teachers, side with his wife and Ross finds himself a minority of one among his colleagues. Although written in novel form this story is based upon experiences of many school teachers amalgamated into few characters. The author has chosen this form to demonstrate the effects of modern education upon students, teachers and administration.

Although the author is not and has never been a school teacher he has been a student in many different settings and schools. His parents were both school teachers as was his wife and both her parents. One set of parents were liberal democrats and the other conservative republicans yet both sets of parents recognized and wrestled with the problems of modern education.

Acknowledgments

Although Jan Williams, my wife Ilene, Oliver DeMille and others have provided invaluable suggestions to improve this story I alone am responsible for the contents. My son Caleb is the photographer for the book cover and my son Eric did much to help with the computer work.

ONE

Frustration gnawed at Ross' vitals as he struggled to continue his lecture in the face of a constant barrage of chattering designed to nettle him. Many of the high school kids on an individual basis were likable enough people but once they began to make what they considered funny remarks, all joined in to make his job nearly impossible. The innuendos made concerning his physical appearance were just vague enough to avoid being outright rude. His students had learned just how far they could go in their game and still not get into trouble.

Trouble, what a joke. Everyone in the room knew that punishment was restricted to the point where there was really no threat to anyone. Normally the students restrained their fun, but today they seemed to be following the lead of one hulking boy in the back row. Over the weeks, Blake had shown an increasing disdain for his short, rounded teacher. Ross had heard snide remarks concerning his thick-lensed glasses; frog eyes, fish eyes and other numerous derogatory remarks, but always whispered when his back was turned.

Lately, the remarks had turned crude. Ross turned to write on the blackboard as he continued speaking.

"Now, we are going to examine and discuss the differences and the similarities between the

French and the American Revolutions and their affects upon the history of . . . . ."

A large book crashed into the wall near Ross' head. He carefully laid down his chalk and turned to face the class.

Blake sat with arms folded, his face a study in amused defiance. He glanced around to assure himself that he had the support of the other students. There was much anticipation on the admiring faces.

There was no question in anyone's mind that control of the class was to be determined at this point. Ross' mild, patient manner had encouraged Blake until he had gained the confidence to issue this challenge.

"Blake, you have lost the privilege to attend this class for two weeks," Ross informed him.

"Would you like to step out in the hall and see who loses their privileges?" Blake countered, standing, drawing himself to his full six foot, five inch height and hitching his pants up over his bulk.

Ross walked to the door and held it for Blake. The soft bang made by the closing door was immediately followed by a solid thump from the hall. Once again the door opened and Ross entered, drawing out his comb and smoothing his short, thinning hair. The students toward the front of the class got a glimpse of Blake with eyes closed, resting peacefully on the hallway floor.

"Is there anyone else?" Ross asked.

A stunned silence was the only reply.

Ross bent and picked up the beautifully illustrated history book and examined the broken binding. He sighed as he placed the book on his desk. It was going to be a long day; it was only the second period of the day.

Before lunch, the vice-principal opened his door and beckoned.

"Careful, Ross, there is going to be hell to pay for this one," he warned as they walked down the hall together.

"Thank you for coming in Ross," Principal Grey greeted him cautiously. "May I introduce Mr. Hastings? He is with the state social services."

"Mr. Hastings, this is Ross Babco."

"Mr. Babco. As you may have assumed, I am here in connection with the incident that took place in your classroom this morning."

Ross checked his watch. Little more than an hour had passed. He nodded his head in the affirmative.

"Mr. Babco, we are long past the era of administering corporal punishment in the classroom. It is contrary to the laws of the state and the policy of this school. Furthermore, the boy's parents are threatening to sue the school district for allowing one of its teachers to abuse their child."

"Have you ever seen this so-called child?" Ross asked.

"What he looks like makes little difference as far as I am concerned," Mr. Hastings countered.

"This 'child' stands head and shoulders above me and is twice my bulk. With great relish he was about to stomp me into the carpet!" Ross exclaimed.

"I don't think you understand the seriousness of the situation."

"On the contrary, you are the one who doesn't understand the seriousness of the situation," Ross returned.

"Well," Mr. Hastings huffed, "I can see we are wasting our time here." He turned his head away indicating Ross could be dismissed.

Principal Grey nodded his head. "You may go, Ross."

At lunch Ross sat with the other history teacher, Robert Handling, who taught the same classes as himself. The two men were as different as two men could be both in physical build and in temperament. Robert was tall, with sloping shoulders, flat stomach, wide hips, and a large plump rear. Ross on the other hand, was short with broad, heavy shoulders and roundness to his belly. Robert's humor was sarcastic and cutting, while Ross was good-natured and mild.

Several of the other faculty members were sitting at the table with them as they finished eating and rose to their feet.

Robert reached over and patted Ross' belly.

"Starting to stick out there a little aren't we, Ross?" he teased as the other teachers chuckled.

"I push mine, you pull yours," he countered, to the glee of the others.

The remainder of the day went quietly enough due to the oft repeated story of Blake's sudden and unexpected demise. Ross cleared up the work on his desk, walked out, and waited in the car for his wife to finish her work. She had loved her job from the very first and had always given more than was required. He had never really known what he would have preferred to do for a living and had majored in education merely as a quick way to get a degree, always hoping that some great opportunity would present itself to save him from having to actually take a teaching job.

Over the sixteen years he had been teaching he had learned to be a good teacher and even come to enjoy watching individual students strive to excel and later go on to be happy, successful people; particularly those who had been labeled slow and had been placed in his Special Ed. classes.

The happiest time of his life had been the first years that he and his wife had worked together in the same school. It was only in the most recent years that a vague dissatisfaction had begun to creep in.

The sight of his trim little wife, Julia, emerging from the large front doors of Cleveland

High brought his thoughts to another subject. He recalled when he had first met her, and the weeks that had passed before he had worked up the courage to ask her out. Neither had been dating anyone else, leaving him with the feeling that she had accepted only because it was a date, not because of any interest in him personally.

He had continued to ask; she to accept, until they had become friends. She displayed a lively sense of humor in a slightly cynical bravado to disguise a timid, sensitive nature. First he fell in love with her large, expressive, intelligent brown eyes and later her romantic spirit. Her bony, angular, fragile body would never be considered sexy but she had succeeded in capturing his heart and soul. He had proposed.

Saying that she was unsure of her feelings, she had put him off for months. Later she had a minor operation on her toes that gave her the excuse of postponing the answer by saying she couldn't make a decision until she was in good health.

Ross had hidden the hurt knowing full well that she hoped for a man more like the image of the husband she had cultivated in her mind all of her young adult life. With the passage of time it became ever more evident that Ross might possibly be the only man to fall in love with her.

"How was your day, dear?" he asked as she set her pile of books on the seat between them, and slid in.

"Not as exciting as yours, from what I hear."

"Oh? And what did you hear?"

"That you have been beating up on the children."

"Poor little buggers."

She chuckled, but then added, "Don't be too flippant. This could be serious."

Ross started the car and pulled away from the curb.

"Today was the most relaxed, peaceful day I've had in years," Ross stated.

"How can you say that? Don't you care what happens to your job?"

"I meant in the classroom. After what happened to Blake, I sensed a little fear in the students. Suddenly, everyone was a little unsure of me, didn't want to upset me. Maybe I should have done this years ago and lived off my reputation."

"Years ago you may have gotten away with it but not today. Besides I don't think fear is the key to good discipline."

"Respect then."

"Violence is not necessary for good discipline either. I have never used violence or intimidation, but I don't have a discipline problem."

Ross knew this to be true. He had lost the debate, but still there was something missing. Even the experienced teachers that in previous years had not had problems were having a more difficult time.

       The garage door slid noiselessly up to allow Ross to pull in next to the other late model car. Their home was a solid cozy brick, with steep roofs to shed the snow. It was warm in winter, cool in summer. The small yard was carefully manicured with many varieties and colors of flowers during the warm season. During the cold season, while Julia was in school and the days were short, the flower gardens usually lay under snow and needed little or no attention.

       Ross had tried to get interested in several different hobbies over the years but had never found anything that had really become important to him.

       At the present time he was a volunteer driver for the ambulance. He had begun to take the EMT courses. Most of his work consisted of driving patients from the local hospital to the larger hospitals in the distant cities when a specialist was required, but rarely did he drive in an emergency situation.

       The interior of their home was carefully and tastefully done, designed to accommodate small parties, according to the desires of his wife. Four or five times a year, Julia invited a few of the faculty members in for an evening.

Ross and Julia entered the house and began the nightly ritual; Ross made the salad and set the table while Julia prepared the main dish. After dinner, Julia spooned two bites of ice cream out of the carton for dessert, but Ross didn't eat dessert in the evening, in an effort to control his weight. Julia cleared the table and loaded the dishwasher while Ross watched the news. Later on, he would put the clean dishes away.

The rest of the evening would be spent reading, playing Scrabble, or sometimes grading papers. Julia was still romantic and spent hours reading romance novels, but there was little passion in their intimate life, although there was no indication that she thought it anything but pleasant. He had often wondered if it would have been different if she had been madly in love when she had married.

TWO

That night after Julia was asleep, Ross was plagued with a growing restlessness. He knew that in the eyes of most people, his life would be considered mundane and yet he had not been unhappy. There had been unhappy experiences in his life. His first born, was a still born boy. The next two pregnancies ended early. The second even earlier than the first, as if Julia's frail, little body had only the strength to make three tries, each more feeble than the last. She had suffered the pains of birth, the after pains, and even the discomfort of producing nourishment, but never the joy of a child.

They had briefly discussed adoption but by that time Julia lacked the will to even sustain the thoughts long enough to provoke action.

Later in the night Ross slept so lightly that he knew that he was dreaming. A huge hour glass with no bottom was ever so slowly leaking the sands of his life upon a flat desolate landscape. He saw himself trudge steadily through the sand and approach the distant horizon just as the last of the sand leaked through the narrow opening and fell upon the ground. A light wind sprang up and obliterated his tracks, even as he disappeared into the distance.

The following day only his long experience and intimate knowledge of his subjects allowed him to go through the motions of teaching, with little alteration from his normal performance.

He sat listlessly at his desk after lunch and watched his Special Ed. class trickle in, one at a time. The students ranged through all grades, from freshmen to seniors. Their abilities also covered the whole spectrum from brilliant to severely handicapped. All had problems adjusting to school life and none were getting good grades in their other classes.

"Hi, Mr. Babco!" a sweet little voice sang out.

"Oh, hi, Missy," he answered absently.

He watched her take her seat nearby and immediately began talking with her neighbor. Her given name was Melissa. She was a senior, a cheerleader, very well liked and almost always cheerful. She struggled conscientiously with her school work but never quite seemed to be able to grasp the concepts. Ross, on occasion, had given her a grade that she had not quite earned to allow her to continue on the cheer leading squad. In this case he couldn't agree with the policy to curtail the student in one area for lack of ability in another. He had a lot less patience with those with ability, who put forth no effort.

Todd, manager for the athletic teams greeted Ross casually. He loved sports but had never made any of the teams. Todd loved to talk and exercised

11

this talent on Missy until the bell rang, and Ross waved him to his seat.

"Today we are going to start on a new program that has been approved for use in Special Ed. classes. To begin with, we will have a test." This statement was met with a groan.

"The first and shortest part of the test will be like any other. There will be right and wrong answers. There will be no whispering or help from anyone. This part of the test will be handed in at the end of class. The second part of the test will consist of giving your opinions or telling about your personal lives. You may take as long as you like. You may take it home for the remainder of the week if you desire. Remember, there are no right or wrong answers but it will do me no good or you any good if the answers are not your own."

Ross passed out the tests and sat back down at his desk. Ten minutes into the class period, the door opened, and a tall, willowy brunette sauntered into the room. Her hooded, dark brown eyes were as beautiful as they were watchful. Her features were nearly perfect, except for the mouth that habitually turned down with disdain for everything and everybody. In the year and a half that she had been in Ross' class, he had only seen her smile three or four times. At such times, she was transformed into one of the most attractive people he had ever seen.

She had the reputation of being mean but she had never been anything but polite to Ross. She was not well liked and no one messed with Olivia. He handed her the test without any explanation. Ross noticed that her expression was less severe today.

Forty short minutes later, Olivia stood and brought the test forward and set it on his desk.

"May I go?"

Ross glanced quickly through the pages and could see that she had considered each answer. Each blank was filled with her large neat script.

Although it was contrary to school policy to be out of the classroom during school time, Ross realized that she would have to sit with nothing to do and for no good reason.

"You may."

By the way that the instructions were written on the test it was assumed that at least four hours would be required for most students to complete it and that rare would be the student that would achieve more than sixty-six percent on the graded portion.

The other students looked up with dismay as Olivia walked out.

Ross used the last few minutes of the class to correct her test. He wasn't a bit surprised when her score was nearly perfect, or had he been surprised the week before when he had recorded her score of thirteen percent on a much easier test. He had come to understand that she lived on an emotional roller coaster, although there was never more than slight evidence recorded on her face of the internal turmoil. Her performance in school, day by day, was an excellent barometer of her shifting moods.

Ross watched Missy's struggle with the test clearly displayed upon her face, in deep concentration and consternation. Missy's good humor and constant cheerful disposition, coupled with her friendly social skills, her blonde, blue-eyed, baby doll good looks and trim agile little body, made her a favorite with the boys, if not all the girls.

Todd, too, had been blessed with a pleasant, easy personality and a sense of humor that he used well to deflect the abundance of rough humor that came his way from the more athletic boys of the school. Todd was short with heavy legs and slow ponderous movements.

These were Ross' favorites, although he liked a good many of the young people in the school. He had never been able to put his finger on the reason for his partiality towards Olivia.

Ross received word from the Principal's office requesting a conference at the end of the school day.

"Come in Ross," Principal Grey motioned him to a chair.

Ross made himself comfortable.

"It has cost me the good part of the day, but I have managed to calm the waters to a marked degree. I have been able to persuade Blake's parents to not sue the school district. Once I had this accomplishment to present to Mr. Hastings, along with your otherwise excellent record, and of course pointing out there were extenuating circumstances, he too was appeased to some degree."

Ross understood from this familiar approach that the principal had struck a deal and that Ross would be required to comply.

"I appreciate that," Ross murmured his thanks.

"Of course, I had to assure Blake's parents that he could return immediately to class, and that nothing like this would ever happen again."

"Of course," Ross acknowledged. "It won't work," he added.

"Now Ross, consider your position, not to mention mine and all the other teachers in the district."

"Alright Wayne, let's consider my situation for a moment. If Blake comes back to class immediately, he will correctly perceive that I do not have the authority to carry out my punishment. He will perceive that I have been punished by my superiors and that he can, with impunity, cause all the disruption he pleases. He will continue to portray himself, to the powers that be, as the victim. This new development will not escape the other students. I will lose all respect and control in that class. The same spirit can't help spill over into the entire school and eventually the entire district."

"Let's suppose that I made the decision to keep Blake out of your class for two weeks. What do you suppose could be the worst scenario?"

"The school district would be sued."

"We've been sued before. It's always hard to determine how these cases are going to turn out, but I'm sure we could survive it."

"I guess we could lose our jobs."

"If we can't work things out between us, the superintendent would have to deal with the parents and the courts. I think my job would be safe."

"Are you willing to let me take the risk?"

"It's not that simple. Whatever else happens, we must satisfy the state. The state will see to it that school in this district continues even if it requires a new teacher, principal or superintendent."

"You could put him in Robert's class," Ross suggested reluctantly.

"I've thought of that. I don't want to."

They both knew and understood that Robert, with his superior intellect and sharp tongue would discipline Blake by destroying him in the eyes of his fellow students, bit by agonizing bit until he would have no influence to cause rebellion or disruption. Along with the destruction of his self-esteem would go the opportunity to be a successful student and maybe the chance to be a successful person.

"I appreciate your dilemma. I will abide by your decision," Ross stated. "Let me know." He began to rise.

"Thank you Ross. You've helped me in my resolve. It is better to sacrifice one student than the morale of the entire school."

"It shouldn't have to be this way."

"I know. It can't be helped."

THREE

So many of the students in his Special Ed. class were having problems with the test that Ross relented and gave them an extra day in class to complete the first part. Olivia was given the next assignment of her regular curriculum to occupy her time. She spent ten minutes on it, then stretched her long, slim, denim-clad legs before her and placed her arms behind her head and stretched. The thin material of her blouse did little to hide her fully developed womanly shape.

Ross looked away in embarrassment. If she could have this effect upon him, he wondered what the effect was upon the other teenagers in the class. She was only seventeen. He couldn't tell if she had done it innocently or not.

When he glanced back, she hadn't changed position but had quit stretching and was not so provocative. She was watching Todd fiddle with some toy.

"Todd, what are you doing?" Ross asked.

The toy immediately disappeared.

"Nothing," Todd replied as innocently as he could.

"Olivia, what are you doing?"

"Helping Todd."

18

The other students burst into laughter at his expense. Olivia had bested him one more time. To add insult to injury, he couldn't help laughing himself.

That evening as he sat watching television he told Julia about the incident.

"I don't know why you put yourself out to help the snooty little cat. You let her get away with murder and even encourage her to show off and be disrespectful."

"She never says a word if I just leave her alone," Ross answered.

"That's just it. You can see what she is doing with her life and can't leave her alone. Remember that time last year outside the gym before the basketball game?"

He did, very clearly. Olivia had been standing in the shadows smoking one of those long, slim, dark brown cigars. She had lowered it from her mouth and concealed it in her hand, not in an effort to deceive him, but more as a polite gesture. She knew he disapproved.

"Olivia," he had spoken sincerely, "it really hurts my feelings to see you using those. They are a mortal enemy to beauty and you are a very lovely young lady."

"And I really like what you taught me about John Locke in history class," Olivia retorted.

19

Ross had felt the heat rise in his face and knew that it had turned red. He turned quickly away.

"What did she mean?" Julia had asked as they had walked away.

"Hard to say," he had answered.

"You understood her perfectly."

Ross had sighed. There was no point in denying it.

"John Locke said, 'It is the total duty of all men to mind their own business.'"

"Do you?" Julie brought him back to the present.

"Yes, yes, I remember," Ross admitted.

"I don't know why you put up with her sass."

"OK," Ross got the attention of the students sitting in a circle, "this is the way this new program is going to work. Each day we will take a different aspect of each of our lives and discuss it in front of the class. By this method we can get to know each other better to help us be more understanding, to see each other's point of view, to share inner feelings and bring us closer together. Everyone will have the opportunity to participate. Now let's work together and make this a good positive experience. This is new to me too.

Today we will imagine that each one of you is a house. We will start with the person on my left. Each one of you will describe what kind of house she is."

Missy was the first to be described as a house. She beamed as each described her as an elegant mansion or a cute little cottage. As they moved around the circle the comments were generally favorable to each person. Todd received a few negative comments on what kind of house he was, but he defended himself with a funny remark and the awkward moment passed.

"We have enough time to describe Olivia before the bell rings."

"Victorian mansion," declared the boy sitting next to Missy. He received some raised eyebrows at his comment.

"That's right," he defended, "a Victorian mansion with gables and turrets, old, dilapidated, isolated, and, of course, haunted."

"With bats," added the next person.

"And an attic full of guano!" chimed in another.

Each tried to outdo the last in adding gruesome details to Olivia as a house.

It was at this point Ross decided to add himself into the experiment.

"Olivia is a solid built brick home designed to keep out the cold and heat, to keep safe those that live within. Unpretentious, but carefully and attractively maintained with a warm, private atmosphere."

The bell rang at this point and class was dismissed.

The second day followed a similar pattern. The subject was, "If we were cars, what kind of car would we be?"

"Olivia would be a very expensive car," began the first boy in the circle. He paused for effect.

"long and black and shiny, with real leather upholstery. Very important, always the first in line in parades . . . . to the cemetery!"

"A hearse, right on!" cried the next in line.

"With embalming fluid for perfume!"

"Driven by grey-faced old men!"

Once again Ross felt compelled to take part although the teacher's guide clearly stated that the teacher was to remain silent. He knew that Olivia, each night after school, wove rugs on her mother's loom to help support the family and to provide for her own needs.

"Olivia is a new four-wheel drive pickup with clean, strong lines. Not only do people notice as she drives down the street but she is capable of hauling heavy loads over long distances or rough terrain."

The following day the subject dealt with the profession each would work.

Todd's imagined profession was clown.

Missy was to be an actress.

"I think Olivia will be a famous cook. She will be known all over the world as inventive and subtle as Lucrecia Borgia," opinioned the first boy.

"Lady of the night," declared the second.

Once again, one derogatory remark after another was expressed around the circle. Suddenly everything went quiet. Todd laughed into the silence.

Casually Olivia had held up a piece of paper for everyone to see. Her sitting immediately to Ross' right prevented him from noticing at first. He held his hand out and she docilely placed the paper in his hand.

Beautifully drawn was the subject that artists consider the most difficult to draw, the human hand. So expertly was it done that Ross readily recognized it as Olivia's own, with the long, tapered fingers and carefully manicured nails. The fingers were casually folded down with the exception of the middle finger which was fully extended.

Ross crumpled the drawing and tossed it in the wastebasket. Olivia had purposely chosen to interrupt just before Ross was to speak. The bell rang.

"Wait!"

Olivia's sharp command stopped the rush to the door.

"Class has not been dismissed, you ill-mannered jerks."

"Sit down," Todd supported Olivia.

When the class looked to Ross for confirmation he nodded his head. He understood at this moment that Olivia was desperate to hear the positive things that he had always said about her.

"Olivia," he began, "is an entrepreneur. She has a self-reliant and resilient nature and will survive in any situation whether the economy is good or bad. Already her work is sold through shops that are known for selling the most expertly crafted products. Her mother and younger brothers can safely depend on her, as will her future family."

Ross made arrangements for an aide to come in and take charge of his next class.

"What do you know about this new program we have in Special Ed.?" he asked the principal once they were comfortably seated.

"Not much. I glanced over it briefly. It seemed like a good concept. Lets the students open up and share their ideas, break down barriers, help them be more understanding of one another."

"Did you think it would work when you read the theory?"

"Quite frankly, I didn't spend much time on it."

"Where did you come up with this program?"

"It's federally mandated."

"Let me tell you how it works in practice. Those that are popular are continually praised and built up until their vanity blinds them to their real worth. They begin to think that they are inherently better. Those that are less popular are taught that they are second class citizens and those that are disliked are criticized and made fun of until what little self-esteem they have is totally obliterated.

"The most important thing in their life becomes centered on what they hear in class. Both the popular and the unpopular alike become very desirous to receive the approval of the group."

"I understand that is the purpose of the exercise. It is then the responsibility of the teacher to guide the thinking of the class to use this influence to mold the student."

"After only three days of criticism Olivia was so desperate for the few words of praise she received from me that she wouldn't let the kids leave before I had my turn. Todd stuck up for her because he understood somewhat the things she had suffered."

"Don't you see that now is the time that you can have a great influence upon these two kids? I think that is just what the program is supposed to do."

"I see that one plump, partially blind, balding man twice their age will never have enough influence to counteract the influence of thirty kids their own age. I won't put those kids through that one more day!"

"You know Ross, I get the feeling there is a little more to this reluctance of yours than is visible on the surface. Why are you so sensitive on this subject?"

"Do you remember when we were in school there were those students that attended remedial reading and remedial English?"

"Sure."

"We call it Special Ed. now. Remember how they were passed from grade to grade and graduated with their age group?" Ross' question was answered with an affirmative nod.

"Wayne, I was trained from a very early age to believe that I was inferior in mental ability. I believed this until I was out of high school. I don't remember what triggered the thoughts, but I do remember thinking that I was fed up with being told I didn't have the ability to succeed. I taught myself to read AFTER I graduated. While I was learning to read, I worked and paid for my schooling and earned a B.S. degree in education."

"That is why you received a minor in Special Ed."

"Yes. I feel strongly that this program is an experiment on children that have been labeled failures, a group considered unsalvageable, of little worth. The program is rotten. It will be hard enough for these kids without this heaped upon their heads."

"I really have very little to say in this matter as it stands. I can only take it up with the school board. Is it a firm decision then that you will not teach this program?"

"Yes."

"I think you are making a big mistake, Ross." Wayne gave Ross time to reconsider but Ross sat silent. "The school board meets before the Christmas break. I'll let you know immediately what they decide."

FOUR

Laughter, yelling and the sound of feet in a hurry, mixed with the general babble of voices outside Ross' room, went unnoticed as he sat at his desk too stunned to collect his thoughts. Quickly the noise subsided until the school became unnaturally quiet. Everyone had left for the holidays and still Ross sat unmoving except for the slight tremble of his hand that held an official looking document.

"Ross?" a tentative voice called from outside his door.

"Ross?" Julia's muffled voice called again, accompanied by the click of the doorknob on a locked door as she tried to get in. Absently Ross got up and opened the door.

"Oh, there you are." Julia had begun to walk away. Ross turned back inside and began to gather the few things from the room that were his personal belongings.

"What are you doing? Ross . . . what's wrong?"

Ross stopped what he was doing and handed her the document, then turned back to his work.

"Terminated!?"

"Fired is the more common term," Ross explained stoically.

Julia continued to read, mumbling the words as she went.

"Insubordination . . . refusal to abide federally mandated programs . . . unnatural affection for young lady of dubious reputation unbecoming a public servant! . . . sudden propensity to commit acts of violence."

Julia raised her accusing, questioning eyes.

"Olivia," Ross stated.

"I try not to meddle, but I did warn you about her!"

"It had little to do with Olivia. To appear totally justified in doing this to me, they had to drag up every incident in recent history to show what a jerk I am."

"They could have had the common courtesy of confronting you face to face instead of sending this horrible letter."

"Wayne was the one chosen to break the news to me. The letter was to clarify the position taken by the school board."

"It won't be easy for me to come back to work after the holidays."

Ross correctly interpreted this not to mean that she would consider quitting to show her support for him, but rather to make sure he understood that he had made her life uncomfortable. The scandal would reflect negatively upon her.

Ross handed his wife a few of his things and motioned her out the door. He followed and locked up. On his way out of the building he tossed his keys to a custodian who caught them, then examined them perplexed, indicating that word of Ross' dismissal hadn't yet circulated.

The vacation that the Babco's had planned had lost all of its appeal as far as Ross was concerned. His parents had worked in education all of their lives. Ross had the distinct feeling that they would not be a bit sympathetic to the stand that he had made. Julia agreed readily enough to call and beg off with the excuse that Ross wasn't feeling well. It was true, Ross felt like hell. The Babco's avoided the school functions that took place during the holidays, the basketball games, the dances, wrestling matches and Christmas caroling.

Ross lay around the house, feeling more useless and frustrated with each passing day. Sheer boredom drove him out of the house and down to the bowling ally. He bowled with more vigor and intensity than usual, sending the pins flying in every direction, but when he finished the game his score was less than average. No matter, it had felt good.

As he walked down the sidewalk toward his car, he suddenly tensed at the sight of the glow of a cigarette in the deep shadows against the wall.

With eyes averted Ross pretended not to see but walked steadily by as if he thought he were alone.

"Mr. Babco?"

"Olivia, I couldn't see you standing there in the dark," Ross apologized as he turned back toward her.

"I'm sorry you lost your job because of me."

"It wasn't because of you," Ross assured her, even as he wondered how she had known and assumed it was her fault. Had one of the school board members not been as discreet as he should have been or had someone overheard him talking with the principal? Realizing that Olivia had stepped completely out of character to express her feelings to him he knew that she must have been desperate to hear those few words of praise he had uttered from time to time. Many times he had questioned the wisdom of his decision but at that moment he understood that he had taken the only right path.

"What they asked me to do was completely unacceptable. No one should be asked to teach like that."

"I'm sorry you won't be teaching anymore."

"Thank you." The interview was over. Ross continued on to his car.

When Ross let the county know that he was available to drive the ambulance on a permanent basis, his pager began to beep at all hours of the

31

day. His training to become a paramedic was stepped up to where he was attending class on a daily basis. The work and the study were fascinating and Ross had no trouble in getting good grades. The feelings of frustration and stagnation that had begun to plague him vanished. Maybe his dismissal from the school was for the better after all.

Ross struggled up from his sleep and depressed the button on his alarm, but the beeping persisted until he realized it was his pager. By the time he arrived at the garage that housed the ambulance, he knew where the accident was. Two paramedics arrived in time to climb in beside him as he backed out and drove away, with lights flashing. A glance at his watch showed the time to be three twenty-three A.M.

A lone deputy sheriff was at the scene. An expensive late model car with a badly smashed front end rested against a solid cement base holding up a street lamp. The door to the driver's side was flung open. Sitting some distance down the street on the curb was a heavy set, richly dressed, middle-aged man with his head in his hands, rocking back and forth ever so slightly.

"The woman has a badly broken ankle and a severe cut," the deputy informed them. The two paramedics began to work to free her ankle.

"Thank goodness she is unconscious."

Looking over their shoulders, Ross noticed the shapely, blood splattered legs of the attractive thirty-something young lady.

"Ross trot over and see if the guy is alright," one of the paramedics instructed.

It was evident that the car had rounded the corner at much too great a speed and had careened across the street to smash into the light pole, throwing the man out and down the street.

To Ross' horror, he discovered that what the street light was reflecting from down the middle of the man's head was his brain! It was no surprise however to smell that he reeked of liquor.

"Oooooh," he moaned softly to himself as he rocked, "My wife ain't gonna like this. Oooooh, my wife ain't gonna like this," he repeated over and over.

"Don't worry about your wife. All she has is a broken ankle," Ross tried to comfort the injured man.

"That ain't my wife! Ooooooh, my wife ain't gonna like this." As the man once more began his litany he began to slowly topple over backwards. Ross, having sunk to his knees was in a position to catch him and ease him down onto the pavement. His hand came away covered with blood and fluid from the man's brain. Slowly, a puddle began to form on the cement. Ross knew that he was dead but in a panic he tried to yell for help; all that came out was a hoarse croak.

Finally, someone heard him and rushed over to see what the situation was. The paramedics worked on the man briefly, but there was nothing that could be done.

Still on hands and knees, Ross retched violently into the gutter. Pale and shaken, he managed to drive back to the hospital while the other two worked on the woman.

While at the hospital, he had cleaned the blood and gore off his hands and waited listlessly for a ride back to the garage although it was only a very short distance.

He felt the fool as the three of them rode in silence.

"I'm sorry," he apologized, "my mind went blank. I just couldn't think of what to do."

"There was nothing to be done," he was assured.

"I remember the first time I had an experience like that. I felt sick for quite a while. I just knew that I wasn't cut out for this kind of work, and I decided to quit, but somehow I managed to come back and try it again. There are nights when we can relieve suffering and occasionally even save a life. Nothing in this world is so satisfying to me. I'm not saying you ever really get used to that sort of thing but you learn to cope. How was it with you?" the first asked the other.

"About the same, I think everyone that works in this profession goes through it. I actually quit twice, but I kept coming back. Now I don't think I could do anything else."

Ross, feeling somewhat reassured, accepted the days off when he would not be on call. Just before dawn he crawled back into his nice warm bed, next to his nice warm wife and prayed fervently for oblivion which finally came. Once the edge of his exhaustion was blunted, he began to dream.

Over and over the man toppled over backwards to have his blood, brains, and life ooze out onto the sidewalk to form a puddle. Over and over Ross felt the sticky liquid on his hands. Over and over he cried for help, but no one heard, no one came. He awoke crying, sweating, and straining against the horror. He was relieved to find his wife had risen and was in the kitchen preparing breakfast. He was ashamed of his weakness.

With each passing day he became more haggard, the dark circles under his eyes more pronounced. Each night he stayed up late to avoid the dreams that came in early morning. Exhaustion drove him to bed. Once he was rested, the dreams came and sapped his energy. Exhaustion accompanied him throughout the day. Luckily his wife started back to school and had to get up early and was gone when the dreams came.

She fretted over him, nagged him, quizzed him, and wondered why he didn't go back to work.

She threatened to make an appointment with a therapist. She worried at him like a dog worries a bone, but he could not confide in her.

As the day grew closer that he was to report back to work, his dreams became more intense, his depression deeper. In desperation he called in and resigned.

It was suggested that later on he might like to try again. He agreed, but he knew he never would.

The following morning he awoke late to find that he felt reasonably rested. Then with a cautious joy he realized that he had passed the night dream free.

FIVE

Over the smooth curve of the bowling   ball Ross sighted in the pins. Then with smooth, gliding steps and a graceful but powerful sweep of his arm, he sent the ball hurling down the lane.   The anticipated curve didn't develop as he had planned, the front pin was struck smack dab in the middle . . . split. With the next ball, he managed to knock one pin across the lane to topple the last pin for a spare.

"Not bad," a male voice complimented.

"Thank you," Ross acknowledged shortly. He didn't care for the tall spare man that had spoken. It was well known that he was a thorn in the side of the superintendent of schools for the district. At public meetings he asked questions with a smug mysterious air, never offering an answer or explanation.   Then he would sigh and shake his head as if those that didn't understand were simpletons.

"You hear from the district yet?" he asked Ross.

"No, and I don't expect to. Things are cut and dried between us."

"Are they? Aren't they violating a contract signed for a full teaching year?'

"I don't know for certain, but under the circumstances I couldn't care less."

"Would you finish the year if they offered your job back with the understanding that you wouldn't have to teach the sensitivity program?"

Ross found that he missed teaching and recognized that he would go back to teaching under the right circumstances.

"Don, you are always hinting that you know things. If you have some pertinent information concerning me, I'd like to hear it otherwise I'd enjoy finishing my game in peace." Ross called his bluff and turned back to locate his ball.

"I saw your name on a list," Don held out the bait.

"What list?" Ross was irritated at himself for showing interest.

"A list of people that are not to work for any government agency in this county."

"Are you on that list?"

"I am."

Ross didn't like being on a list with Don.

"And where did you get hold of such a list?"

"I keep my ear to the ground." He shrugged. "Of course you understand that they wouldn't want this list published."

Turning away from Don, Ross took his next turn at the pins. He left three standing. When he next looked up, Don was gone.

With an effort, Ross put the strange interview with Don out of his mind, but his enthusiasm for his game quickly subsided. He returned home and puttered about the house. Finding that he was thinking about his students . . . ex-students came as no surprise to him. The piece of pie he found in the refrigerator demanded a big dollop of whipped cream which it got. While savoring his snack, he waked over and turned on his answering machine.

"Ross, Superintendent Bascomb. Would you be so kind as to call me here at the office if you get home before I leave at five? If not I'll call you from home later tonight." Mr. Bascomb's voice was friendly.

Ross called immediately.

"Hello, Ross. So good of you to call. How's the wife?"

"Fine, thank you."

"Good, good. Ross, the school board and I have reviewed the circumstances surrounding your dismissal and have found that some of the evidence turns out to be nothing more than hearsay. We might try to excuse ourselves by saying that it came from what we thought was an unimpeachable source, but we freely admit that we have made a mistake. We should have checked first before putting you through this ordeal. We would like to offer you the opportunity to fulfill your contract with us with no loss of pay whatsoever for the time you have had off."

"And the curriculum of my Special Ed. class?"

"You teach whatever you feel is best."

"Will you have my name stricken off the list?"

"Pardon me?" Bascomb sounded puzzled, but the hesitation had been a little too great.

"He knows!" Ross thought in amazement.

"Never mind. It's not important," he answered aloud.

After the interview, Ross sat and tried to sort things out. Only one conclusion fit the information that he had. Don had blackmailed the school board with the threat of publishing 'the list' if they did not offer to rehire Ross, but why did he do it? Who kept the list and who was on it and to what purpose was it kept?

Some of his colleagues acted as if he had never been gone, others displayed some confusion concerning how they thought they should treat him. Still others made it plain that they considered his stand foolish and that they were disassociating themselves from his rebellion. Despite this mixed reaction, his first day back went well.

"Hey, Mr. Babco, are we going to do that 'What kind of car would I be if I were a car?' stuff?"

"That is called the sensitivity program, and no, we are not going to do that anymore," Ross answered.

Olivia turned her face away but not before Ross saw the smile that changed it from one of sullen disdain to one of bright beauty.

"Mr. Babco?"

"Yes?"

"Rumor has it that you decked Blake back in the fall. Is that true? Nobody saw it." This from Danny fullback on the football team, who weighed in at two hundred twenty pounds.

"I've heard that rumor myself," Ross put him off.

"Do you know karate?" Danny persisted.

"I took a class in self-defense years ago when I was a kid," Ross admitted.

"Show me the move you used to take care of Blake."

"I doubt you need to know that. I'm sure you can take care of yourself," Ross pointed out.

"Todd's been picking on me," Danny retorted.

The class laughed.

"Alright," Ross agreed, beginning to get irritated. "Here are the rules." Ross began to roll up a few pages of the newspaper into two foot long clubs. "You may strike or poke with this only. There will be no other attempt at contact other than this. Is that agreed?"

"Sure."

41

"And I will say when the lesson is over, is that agreed?"

"Sure," Danny grinned.

Ross handed him his weapon. Danny struck instantly, hoping to score, using the element of surprise.

Pop. Ross' weapon landed to the side of Danny's head. Wop, wop, the blows fell on his ears and eyes. The weapon was too flimsy to cause any pain but gave off a resounding noise with each blow. Danny, shielding his eyes with one hand, charged forward swinging with the other. He was poked in the stomach, and then slapped on the fanny as he charged past. He wheeled, not unlike a bull turning on a matador, only to receive more blows about his eyes and ears, his own blows never finding anything but air. Danny's temper began to flare, not because he had been hurt at all but because he felt humiliated.

"Lesson is over," Ross announced.

Danny lowered his defense from his face to find Ross standing on the other side of his desk holding a tattered newspaper. His own carefully rolled newspaper had not even a wrinkle in it. He looked rather angry, but in a short time his good humor was restored.

"Alright," Ross calmed the laughing students down, "we've had our fun, let's get down to work."

Later on in the class everyone was studying quietly as Ross opened his desk drawer and discovered an expensively wrapped box of chocolates. He took the box out and set it on his desk and opened the card.

"Welcome back, Special Ed."

Ross stood before the class. He was surprised at the emotion that welled up in him but he controlled it.

"Thank you. That was very thoughtful." He broke the cellophane and took out a piece. Just as he selected a delicious looking chocolate he noticed a picture of a grasshopper on the box and realized he was about to eat a chocolate covered insect, but he hesitated only for a moment and popped the candy into his mouth. It was crunchy similar to a Butterfinger bar but chocolate was all he could really taste. It was good quality chocolate.

Pretending to not have noticed the looks of anticipation and glee on the faces of many of the students, he started at the head of the first row and offered a chocolate to each student, starting with Missy. She took one before she remembered what they were. Then feeling trapped and not knowing how to get out of her predicament she began to eat. Her color was poor after the first bite.

Each student declined and looked away as he passed smiling down each row.

"Thank you." Olivia was the only one to accept. "Ummm, those are good."

"They are good aren't they?" Ross agreed.

"I think I'll have another." And he did.

"May I?" Olivia reached for another. Ross moved the box closer for her. "Excellent quality."

"Yes, these are terribly expensive."

Ross returned to his desk and put the chocolates away in the drawer.

Later in the day after all of the other kids had gone home, Missy and Todd came to his room to receive extra help with their assignments. Ross, having explained again what needed to be done and demonstrated for them, he walked out into the hall to get a drink of water. Upon his return he discovered that Mrs. Blanchard, one of the custodians, was following a big push broom about the classroom. She was a short, round, dark-haired, dark-eyed woman of middle age. A heavy Welsh accent sometimes made it difficult to understand her, but Ross liked her and always tried to be friendly.

"How are you today?" he smiled.

"Oh, fine, Mr. Babco."

Ross sat down at his desk. Absently, he opened the drawer and reached for a chocolate. There were two or three missing he was sure.

"Mrs. Blanchard, did you try one of these chocolates?"

"Oh, no, Mr. Babco! I'd never take anything from your desk!"

"Would you like to try one? My students gave them to me as a joke but they are quite good. It is the first time I've ever tried chocolate grasshoppers."

Mrs. Blanchard's hand reaching for the candy was arrested in midair at this comment. Her face turned red and she began to emit a choking noise just before she whirled and scuttled out of the room and down the hall, retching every step of the way, leaving the condemning evidence all over the floor.

Missy wrinkled up her nose at the smell.

"Oh, no, Mr. Babco! I'd never touch anything in your desk!" Todd mimicked with a grin. By the look on his face Ross guessed he thought Ross had done it on purpose to catch the custodian in a lie, but Ross felt bad about the whole thing.

Entering the room a while later, Mrs. Blanchard went about her work with head down and eyes averted as she cleaned up her own mess.

Six

Later in the week as Ross and Julia were grocery shopping, Ross heard his name and turned.

"Hello, Don."

"I hear you've gone back to work," Don commented casually, but his eyes were smiling smugly.

"Yes. Don," Ross began hesitantly, "I have a feeling that it was due to some influence that you have with the school board. If so, I'd like to thank you."

"I have less influence with the board than anybody in town. Everybody knows that," Don laughed, but his look of satisfaction deepened.

Look," Ross countered irritably, "I've never enjoyed your innuendos and word games. If a man has something to say let him say it."

"Well, it's obvious that you have something on your mind, so follow your own counsel and say it." Don's own expression hardened.

"Reason tells me that I was reinstated because pressure was put upon the school board by a third party. You were aware that this was going to happen before I was. Therefore the third party is you or you know of them or are associated with them. I alone sit in the middle of this hidden dispute, unaware of what is going on. I don't like it."

"Are you aware of the history of Daniel Oman?"

"Of course."

"He was considered the most famous and influential educator in the history of this state."

"I teach that in my history classes." Ross resented the lecture on history.

"Do your history books include his fight against federal aid to education?"

Ross didn't recall this bit of information and stood silent.

"He often quoted the man known as the Father of the Constitution when federal aid was discussed in the Constitutional Convention. 'If government finances education, the schools will reflect the ideology of the party in power.' Close quote."

"What's that got to do with me?"

"Our present government allows no prayer in school."

"Our Constitution provides for a wall of separation between church and state," Ross argued.

"The Constitution never mentions it. That was a statement made by Thomas Jefferson in the context that religion was to be protected from government, not the other way around."

"I know for a fact that I am right. We just covered this subject in my American history book.

I'll lend you the book if you wish," Ross finished confidently.

"No need. I believe you. If you are really interested in history, read the Constitution and the works of Mr. Jefferson and compare it with your history book."

"You've succeeded in diverting me again," Ross accused.

"Not at all, there are three great religions that are the basis of western civilization: Judaism, Christianity, and the Islamic. Each accepts the Old Testament wherein the creation of the earth is explained. Our government prohibits the teaching of the 'creation' even as a theory, but publishes a list of school books that each school district must choose from. Without exception, the theory of organic evolution is taught as if it were fact. Who is the party in power?"

"All this is connected with my dismissal?" Ross smiled skeptically.

"The program that you were asked to teach was designed to make the students dependent on other people, their instructor and the school system, for their self-esteem, their measurement of self worth, and their success in life. By the time they graduate they will come to believe that man and his institutions are capable of and must solve man's own problems, there is no God. This ideology is called Humanism."

48

"Don, I have worked with these people for years! I know them! They are good people! You will never convince me that they would deliberately set out to destroy our western civilization!"

"I couldn't agree more. I, too, believe that they are good people, but they have been through the sensitivity program themselves. Their lives are still rooted in the western culture, but the next generation is being taught by sincere, capable people who will be all the more effective for all that."

"Don, I want no more help from you. I'll take my own risks and my own punishments!"

"Of course, you've got ninety days left on your contract. Read carefully your own textbooks that you teach from in your own classes. Decide for yourself who is the party in power." Don smiled an enigmatic smile and walked away.

Ross turned to find his wife standing behind him with an angry expression on her face.

"You heard."

"The son-of-a-bitch is nothing but a trouble maker! Everyone knows that! You stay away from him!"

The conversation with Don continued to rankle as it came unbidden to his mind now and again. Don had not answered the questions that Ross desired but had given him some mysterious runaround. These thoughts were distracting Ross somewhat as he stood before his history class.

He noted that one of his students was distracted also. Olivia sat in the rear corner with her elbows on her knees and her wistful face framed in her shapely hands, gazing out the open window at the boys playing softball. The first warm breezes of spring were gently blowing the curtains around her and ruffling her long, dark hair.

A plan formed quickly, came to mind. He would lower his voice as he slowly approached her. He figured that if he droned on with no change of inflection and walked quietly, that he could step into the small space between Olivia and the window before she realized he was there. As he got closer, he saw that her finger would serve as a blinder to keep her from catching movement with peripheral vision.

He expected to have her look up and be embarrassed as the class laughed at her being caught, but as he stepped in front of her, she dropped one hand from her face and leaned to one side and looked around him without even glancing up.

The class did laugh, but the joke was on him instead of her!

"Olivia!" he spoke sharply.

She straightened around in her desk without change of expression.

"What am I going to do with you?" he asked softly as he bopped her gently on the head with his fist. This action brought another outburst of laughter.

Ross returned to the front of the room and asked one of the boys to read a portion of a report that he had handed in that Ross felt was particularly well done. Again Ross' mind wandered as familiar material was covered, but suddenly something caught his attention.

"Paul, read that last statement once more please."

"When our country was first established it was necessary to be an individualist in order to colonize and settle the vast empty land, but now that there are no more physical frontiers, it has become necessary for the government to make decisions based on what is most beneficial for the great mass of the people."

Ross waited until the report was finished, and then asked the students to respond to this statement.

"There has to be some kind of control or people can't live together in crowded conditions," Lyle asserted.

"Our natural resources can't stand the assault that it suffered at the hands of the pioneers. They just went and took what they wanted. If we did that now there would be nothing left," Alan contributed.

51

"I've heard that laws are made to help us be free. I think that laws that are made for the majority make the most people free," Wilma suggested timidly.

A few chuckles greeted something that Olivia murmured.

"Olivia, if you have something to say, speak out." Ross' intention was to quell the interruptions.

"I said," Olivia spoke loudly, "we should all move to mainland China." Ross didn't immediately catch her meaning so she continued. "China, I hear, has more laws than anyone else. If laws make us free then China must be the freest nation in the world," Olivia reasoned sarcastically.

Hands waved in the air.

"Speak frankly," Ross called on a student named Frank.

"Frankly speaking," Frank paused to receive his laugh at this old joke, "you have to have good laws to benefit the majority of the people. That's why the majority of the people in a democracy have the say."

"I pledge allegiance," Olivia stood with hand over heart, eyes raised to the distance and in a mock reverence recited, "to the flag of the United States of America and to the REPUBLIC for which it stands . . ." She sat down.

The bell rang, much to Ross' disappointment.

"Perhaps we should examine the difference between a republic and a democracy in our next class period. Read up on it. I would appreciate all the help I can get on the subject," Ross managed before the kids bolted for the door.

He caught the attention of one of the students and motioned him over.

"Tell me, what did Olivia do to make everybody laugh when I bopped her on the head? I was standing behind her and couldn't see."

"She rolled her eyes around and left them crossed, and she let her tongue flop out."

Ross sat in the peaceful silence and contemplated briefly before his next class filed in. Olivia had certainly begun to emerge from her silent shell, but Ross wasn't sure that he liked it. Her barbed wit was hard to cope with. She had learned that she had a knack of inciting laughter, and he suspected that she enjoyed it immensely although she never let it show. Her attitude toward life seemed to have softened some, letting her feel more at ease to speak out. Ross had encouraged this he knew, but wasn't quite prepared for what he had seen emerging.

She would always be independent and tough minded, but Ross hoped she would be able to complete the transition and become a happier and a more amiable person.

The kids entering for his next class shattered his brief moment of tranquility.

SEVEN

That afternoon after school Ross stopped by Julia's classroom.

"I'm going to be a few minutes in the library," he explained. "If you need to go, I will walk home."

"Norma," Ross spoke to the librarian, "I need a copy of the Constitution."

"There is a copy in the back of your history book."

"Yes, but there is an explanation after each article. I want one just as it was written."

"Sorry we don't have one."

"Hmmm, how about a copy of The Works of Jefferson?"

"Don't have one, but let me check and see if there is one in the state system. If there is I could order it in and get it in two days."

Norma's fingers flew briefly over the computer keyboard.

"There isn't one in the system," she announced after a short wait.

"Try The Works of Benjamin Franklin."

"Don't have that either," Norma informed him after a short wait.

"Washington or Madison?"

"Nope, there are some biographies," Norma suggested.

"When were they written?"

"Ummm let me see. Oh, they are all the latest stuff. Nothing older than four years," Norma stated happily. "Shall I order something for you?"

"No, I guess not." Ross turned to leave.

Julia was still working diligently in her room when he stuck his head in the door.

"Do you know that there is not one of the Founding Father's works in the whole library system of the state?"

"No, I didn't know that," she answered absently as she continued on with her work.

"Don't you find that a little strange?"

"I guess." Her tone of voice indicated she wasn't interested.

"Let me ask you something," Ross tried again.

"Let me finish up here. You can ask me on the way home."

"How much longer will you be?"

"Fifteen, twenty minutes."

"I'll walk."

The warm sun and the cool air were invigorating, but the events of the day tugged at Ross' mind until the pleasures of spring were forgotten by the time he reached home. Julia pulled into the garage and entered the house just ahead of him.

Ross remained silent as they went through the nightly ritual preparing supper.

"Julia," he finally could keep silent no longer, "do you think there is still room for individualism in America?"

"Of course."

"The history book that I teach from doesn't agree. It says that individualism was necessary in the settling of our country, but now we need to conform to laws that will benefit the great mass of the people."

"I'm sure that is true as far as governmental responsibility goes but there is still room for personal preferences that don't infringe upon anybody."

"I find that very interesting how you did that," Ross told her.

"Did what?"

"Did a flip flop in your thinking as soon as you discovered what I was referring to."

"Are you criticizing me?"

"No. I merely observe how loyal you are to your profession. You didn't even stop to think but made your defense automatically."

"What's got into you? Have you been talking to Don again?"

"No, but I have been taking the time to observe more closely."

"Observing what?"

"Never mind," Ross declined to answer, seeing Julia was in no mood to discuss the subject. "I hear you had a disturbance in your class today," he changed the subject.

"It wasn't much of a disturbance," Julia downplayed the incident. "It was over with before anyone really had a chance to react. He didn't jerk his pants down until he was already opening the door. It was just a flash and then he was out the door."

"What are they going to do to him?" Ross wondered.

"He has been suspended for two days."

"Two days? If I had mooned a class of female majority when I was in school they would have thrown me out permanently, not to mention the fact that my parents would have grounded me until I was thirty-five!"

"The boy's parents think the punishment is too harsh."

"No! That explains why the kid is such a mess."

"Actually, he has been one of my best behaved students."

"And you claim you don't have a discipline problem!" Ross exclaimed.

"I don't. This was an isolated incident," Julia defended coldly.

"Tell me something. Haven't the differences between what the schools were like when we were young and the schools of today given you cause for concern, even alarm?"

"Not at all. I think that the students are more open and are treated on more of an equal basis than when we went to school. Sometimes it is quite refreshing."

"I have to agree that teachers and students are more equal, but the students haven't risen to the level of self-restraint that the teachers have. The teachers have been forced to deal down on their level."

"I think that kids are more intelligent and responsible than we were. Not all of them of course, there were plenty of ne'er-do-wells around in my day too," Julia argued.

"The good kids are better; they have to be just to survive. The bad kids are worse and this segment is growing rapidly. Still, the majority of the kids are drifting along in imitation or reflection of our society in general."

"So if they are like the rest of society, how can you blame it on the school?"

"I don't see how the schools can do anything but reflect the culture that they are a part of, especially in the unique position that they occupy."

"What do you mean?"

"Well, they are funded with public money. The employees are licensed by the state. Both the state and the people at large keep an eye on what happens. The policies and curriculum must please most of those involved or there are confrontations and major disturbances. Most people shun this kind of interaction. They like things to go along as smoothly as possible."

"Am I right in thinking that you believe that the schools are compounding this cultural drift, so called, because they are an intricate and important part of the culture itself?"

"Yes."

"And what is your solution to this?"

"I don't know. My uneasiness is based more on instinct or feelings than anything concrete."

"Then you, by your own admission, are just drifting like you accuse everybody else of doing. You have no right to criticize until you can identify the problem and propose a reasonable solution. I think you are resentful of the way you were treated by the school board, but you said yourself that people don't like troublemakers that get out of step with society. If you would adjust your attitude and accept the fact that your troubles are your own, your sense of purposelessness would melt away." Julia delivered her opinion as she left the kitchen. Ross understood that she was tired of the subject and didn't want to hear his rebuttal.

She was right about one thing. He needed to identify the problem and study it out carefully in his mind until he found a solution, or he would be guilty of nothing less than murmuring, which was a complete waste of time.

Ross loaded the dishwasher, went into the den, and sat next to his wife in the love seat as she watched the T.V. He pulled off his shoes and put his arm around Julia's shoulders with the intent of drawing her near. It was their custom to sit under a warm afghan together on nights that were chilly.

Julia, resisting his gentle tug, continued to sit straight rather than relax against him.

"What's the matter?" Ross asked.

"'What's the matter?' he says," she said to herself. "You sat and criticized me all during dinner, and then you come in here and want to be cozy like nothing was ever said."

"I thought we were discussing the merits of the school system in our present culture. How is that construed as my being critical of you?" Ross quizzed her, but she ignored him, her eyes fixed on the T.V.

Some time later as Julia rose to leave the room, Ross clicked off the T.V. with the remote and began to follow her.

"Still mad?"

"Don't you understand? Teaching is everything to me. I love the kids, and the school, and the dances, and the football games. If it weren't for these things there would be no excitement and satisfaction in my life."

Later in the week Ross reluctantly called Don and asked if he knew where to find the works of the Founding Fathers. It came as no surprise when he received several suggestions. By the end of the day, the material was in his hands. He made it a point to look up those topics that corresponded with those being taught in the history book that he used in school. He was stunned at the differences between what Thomas Jefferson actually said, and what he was reported to have said in the modern history.

Next, Ross checked the references and the footnotes to try and discover what research the modern text was based on.   The names of the researchers and the titles of previous works were cited.   In response to some vague memory, Ross went into the attic and dug out his old high school history book. It was one of the works cited as a reference.   It too cited previous researchers and references. Over the next several days, Ross traced the sources back through one generation of textbooks after another until he arrived at the works of the founding fathers.

The only conclusion was that modern text books were founded on the old, but over the years they took on a meaning, in many cases, in total contrast to what had actually taken place.   He mentioned this to Julia.

"As more research is done, more things come to light," was her explanation.

"What do you think of this?" Ross began summarizing his reading. "Thomas Jefferson was opposed to the bank as set up under Secretary of the Treasury, Alexander Hamilton. Later on, Hamilton recognized that Jefferson was right, but by that time the bank had great power and influence. Andrew Jackson was hailed as a great hero by great patriots of the day for getting rid of the bank. Abraham Lincoln warned his generation against re-instituting such a bank. This view prevailed through the administration of William McKinley but in about 1916, the bank was voted back into existence. The history book I teach out of calls Andrew Jackson a fool for ousting the bank."

"Hasn't it occurred to you that with our modern technology and advancement that we might possibly have a learned a better way?"

"If that is true, then why do historians not record history instead of inserting their own opinions? It appears to me that in this century, history books were more intent on molding public opinion than in recording history."

"Its talk like that that will push you right of the system, and you will have nobody to blame but yourself," Julia asserted.

"We claim that we are teachers. Are we afraid to even look at ourselves?"

"Let me show you something." Julia rummaged through a large book bag that was usually so full of books she could hardly carry it. "There, read that," she demanded. "You are always quoting Daniel Oman."

Ross took the book and read where his wife was pointing.

"Teaching is the most noble profession. One need not be ashamed to be ignorant for we are all ignorant in some way, but to remain ignorant is the greatest tragedy."

Julia reached out and took back the history of the state. The quote was in the title page and extolled Daniel Oman as the greatest educator. She wore a little smile of triumph.

"He also said, '. . . that to not get a formal education is not the worst thing that can happen to a person," Ross countered.

EIGHT

Threading his way through the crowd, Ross gained his seat in the section of the auditorium he was assigned to supervise. Many of the towns-people had come to mingle with the students in order to hear the Honorable Senator Willis Lanbaum speak.

The Senator was very popular and had already served eighteen years. He was considered unbeatable in his position as one of the national conservative leaders. Ross had voted for him in the past and intended to do so again in the fall when he came up for re-election. By the nod of heads around him during the speech, Ross knew that many of the people assessed it the same way that he had. He enthusiastically joined in the applause at the end of the speech. The audience was then invited to ask questions of the Senator which he fielded with experience and skill. Most were asked by the student body and dealt with his personal experiences as a public servant.

As interesting as Ross found this insight into the circles that the Senator traveled in, his interest increased as he became aware that Olivia was standing and waiting her turn to be recognized.

"Senator," she began in a strong, steady voice, "what is your opinion of George Bush's 'New World Order' and do you think that Bill Clinton will continue with it?"

"First, let me say this. Some people believe that the 'New World Order' is a one world government, but this is not true. It is merely a group of nations that have agreed to help police the world, as the United States is tired of and no longer capable of policing it by herself. I am sure that Mr. Clinton will support the 'New World Order'."

"Senator," continued Olivia as she was still standing, "I believe it was George Washington that said 'Government is not eloquence but force,' clearly indicating that government is nothing more or less than police power. For a group of nations to assume police power, they assume governmental authority, which is by definition a one world government. I think you understand this as well as I do. I cannot in good conscience vote for you," Olivia finished and sat down.

The Honorable Senator was obviously stung by the implication that he had deliberately set out to deceive the people with the answer that he had given, not to mention the fact that he indeed supported the 'New World Order', but he responded smoothly.

"I respect your opinion, young lady, but I believe that I understand the functions of government a little better than you do. Are there any other questions?"

The meeting was brought to a close shortly thereafter with no lessening of the applause that the Senator received, indicating that Olivia's comments were not considered of any great importance. Ross had felt pride in the fact that Olivia had exhibited a poise and maturity beyond her years, but he wondered at the direction her questions had taken. It had taken certain courage to suggest that the Senator was deliberately deceiving the people when the people themselves were so in favor of his being returned to the Senate.

Moving as quickly as he could, Ross moved outside the door and waited for the opportunity to speak with Olivia as she came out. His patience was rewarded; she emerged alone among the crowd.

"Olivia," Ross got her attention and drew her away from the flow of people. "What is the New World Order and why are you so against it?"

Ross became uneasy as he realized that Don had moved up just behind his shoulder and had heard the question.

"Just like the Senator said, there will be an international police force to enforce international law."

"Don't you believe we need international law?" Ross asked.

"Sure, but not the way they want it."

"What other way is there?"

"The way it was when this country was founded."

"Which was?"

"By treaty."

"How is it done now?"

"Through international organizations like the U.N."

"We are members of the U.N. by treaty, are we not?"

"Yes, but that is different."

"How so?" Ross was confidant that he had won his point, for Olivia was increasingly frustrated in her attempt to carry her point.

"The Constitution does not give to its leaders the right of making treaties that violate the constitution itself," Don joined the conversation.

"How does the U.N. treaty violate the Constitution?"

"It provides for the intervention of international troops in the event that the U.S. violates the resolutions made by the international legislature. For example, Iraq was attacked by U.N. peacekeeping forces, the majority of which were American soldiers. Because as George Bush said, the Iraqis were resisting the 'New World Order' . If Americans or any segment of them resist the 'New World Order' by international law, the U.N. forces have the right to invade American soil to discipline the 'Rebels,'" Don explained.

"The way I see it is that the U.N. does on a world wide basis what the Constitution did for the thirteen original colonies," Ross argued.

"I might accept that if the U.N. charter was as noble a document and had been written by as noble of men as wrote the Constitution, but there are some very glaring differences."

"For example?" Ross demanded.

"The Constitution is based upon the premise that all men are created equal by a supreme and just being through whom we get our rights, and that no man may violate those rights. Those rights are carefully listed as are the rights delegated to the government by the people. In contrast, the U.N. does not mention or recognize God in any fashion, not stated nor implied. The charter is so vague and so broad as to give the U.N. the right to anything it can get its members to vote into law. Such an unbridled opportunity for raw power would tempt the best of men, but it wasn't written by good men but men calculating to establish a one world socialist dictatorship."

"I have a hard time believing that," Ross informed Don.

"Are you a Christian?" Don asked.

"I am."

"Lay the two documents side by side, compare them closely and decide which of the two Christ could have written."

"I'm late for class," Olivia excused herself.

"You did a good job exposing the Senator," Don complimented, "I was proud of you."

"Thank you, Uncle Don." Olivia smiled with pleasure as she turned and hurried away.

Standing before the display of a big screen T.V., Ross' mind was occupied, carefully weighing the astronomical price and the need to alleviate the deteriorating situation at home. Julia had stated often enough her desire for the T.V. and had hinted broadly that it would be just the thing to receive as an anniversary present. She had the money to buy it for herself but somehow it had become, in some way that he had never quite understood, proof of his affection for her.

Sighing in resignation, Ross wrote out the check and left instructions on when to have it delivered and set up at home. Saturday morning when the technicians arrived, Julie had gone downtown to do her weekly shopping. The den had already been rearranged Ross noted, indicating that Julia had assumed that she would be getting what she wanted. One short hour later, Ross had everything just as he wanted it.

"Hon," he called as soon as he heard Julia in the kitchen putting away groceries, "come here a sec would you? I'm in the den."

As she walked through the door, Ross hit the switch on the remote. Seemingly the whole wall on the far side of the room burst into life.

"Oh!" Julia exclaimed in delight. "Isn't that wonderful! It's almost like being there." Her hand reached out for the controls. She switched through the channels, stopping for a while to watch the ice skaters. The female partner was petite and pretty with strong, shapely legs. Ross was disappointed when Julia switched again and finally stopped to watch a basketball game.

"The playoffs!" she exclaimed and settled back to watch.

For the new few days, Ross watched one team after another be eliminated until finally a championship team was declared. Quite frankly, he was tired of the newest member of the family and abandoned it and returned to his studies, but Julia spent most of her spare time in the evening relaxing and snacking in front of the huge screen.

Sitting in his library, a small room that had once been decorated as a nursery, Ross discovered a quote in his modern text that was, in it's context, a complete perversion of its original meaning as found in the writings of George Washington. It was apparent to Ross that it had to be deliberately written to conform to the tone of the rest of the chapter. He took the two books and walked into the den to share his find with Julia.

"Listen to this . . ."

"Shhhhh," Julia held up her hand for silence. She hadn't taken her eyes off the screen. The situation comedy was drawing to a close and she didn't want to miss it.

Ross watched briefly to see what could be so interesting, and then turned away in disgust. Irritated at his wife's total lack of interest, he resolved that he would keep his views to himself, but hardly a day passed by that he didn't find something so interesting that he could not help but try to share it. The results were always the same. He even tried insulting her just to get a result different than a detached "Shhhhh."

"You are the skinniest couch potato I've ever seen."

"Shhhhh."

Later he tried to make her feel guilty.

"You know its past time to be cleaning and cultivating the flower beds. They are going to look like hell."

"When did you become interested in flowers?"

"I'm not but you've always . . . . ."

"Then where's the problem?" She turned back to her program.

He made only one more try.

"Tests have shown that all this sex and violence on T.V. isn't good for you."

"I thought you liked sex."

"I do, but a starving man doesn't like to see a bunch of rich, spoiled gluttons pigging out all the time.

Julia gave him a sharp, cold stare and turned abruptly back to her show.

The momentary sense of triumph Ross knew would cost his dearly in the long run, but he had finally made one thrust past her indifference

NINE

Waiting patiently for Wayne to finish up his phone call, Ross sat in the principal's office, wondering what his friend had on his mind.

"Sorry to keep you waiting," Wayne apologized as he hung up the phone. "We have a problem that I felt would best be resolved with your help." Wayne paused and looked at Ross over his glasses.

"If I can," Ross answered, recognizing that Wayne could usually get at least a commitment before even making his request.

"Olivia has been skipping class on a regular basis. P.E. to be more precise. It has come to my attention that she seems to accept you a little more than the other teachers."

"I'll talk to her and see what I can do."

Wayne sat back in his chair and rubbed his chin in the old gesture that Ross was so familiar with.

"You don't think that will be enough," Ross correctly surmised.

"Hmmm, possibly," Wayne responded.

"What else do you want me to do? Spy on her?"

Wayne smiled at Ross like he would a young student who had correctly recited his multiplication tables.

"Her P.E. class does coincide with your free period. However, you handle it anyway you think is best. I sure appreciate this Ross." Wayne had ushered Ross out and had shut the door before Ross realized that the responsibility had been placed upon him without his verbal commitment.

Despite his feelings of resentment, Ross, that very day was stationed to watch the students as they walked from the main building to the end of the block to the P.E. building. Many of the students crossed the street to the little store for a snack, then back across the street to class. Olivia was among this group. She entered the store, but as the students in groups of twos and threes emerged and went to class, Olivia wasn't among them. It was well past time for class to start when Ross walked across the street and glanced in the store.   No Olivia. Thinking that she might have somehow come out of the store without him noticing, he walked back across the street and entered the gym.

"Hello, Rhea.   Did Olivia come to class today?"

"Haven't seen her."

"How about yesterday?"

"Yep."

"And the day before that?"

"Nope."

"Do you mind if I take a look at your roll book?"

The roll book revealed the fact that Monday, Wednesday and Friday Olivia cut class. Tuesday and Thursday she attended faithfully. Ross thanked Rhea and left.

Back at the store, he questioned the store-keeper.

"Ina, is there another exit besides the front door?"

"There is, but its nailed shut."

"May I see it?"

"Come this way."

A close examination of the door made it plain that it hadn't been used for a long time. The dirt in the cracks was undisturbed. The weeds visible through the unwashed pane were untrammeled.

"Still trying to catch Olivia?" Ina asked in obvious amusement.

"Yeah," Ross admitted.

"Last winter they accused me of letting her out the back door although there were no footprints in the snow." Ina let it be known that she was innocent, and that she didn't think much of the previous attempts the school had made in their detective work.

"Is there anything you can tell me that might help?"

"She walks in here and makes her purchases just like anybody else, and she walks right out the front door just like everyone else."

"You don't see which way she goes?"

"You can see how narrow my view is," Ina invited.

Ross looked down the long counter that ran down one side of the long narrow building. Ina's view was indeed very narrow. She would be very busy during the brief time between classes.

Ross decided the next best approach would be to simply ask Olivia where she went, which he did that very afternoon when she walked into class. He motioned her over to his desk.

"Tell me where you go every other day instead of going to P.E."

"Uptown."

"What do you do?"

"Hang out."

"Hang out?"

"Yeah."

"That isn't a very definitive term," Ross pointed out.

"Hanging out isn't a very well defined thing," Olivia countered.

Ross gave it up.

Thursday, Ross watched as Olivia marched dutifully across the street from the store to P.E.

Friday he watched again, and he had Rhea watching the store from the other end of the block. The doorway was in sight every second except for one brief minute while the delivery man stopped the bread van out front and ran in with his order.

As prearranged, Ross called Rhea on the phone.

"Did she show up?"

"Nope."

"Did you see her come out of the store?"

"Nope, I told you that we have tried this before and it didn't work," Rhea reminded.

"Well, let's look at this reasonably. Ina says that Olivia walks right out the front door. I believe her. Besides, there is nowhere else for Olivia to go. The front door is in sight all the time except for the two minutes that the bread van is parked there. From my angle I could see if she came out and went behind the van. From your position you could see if she came out and went in front of the van, but nobody saw her. There was only one place she could have gone, right?"

"Where?"

"INTO the van," Ross cried triumphantly.

"That seems highly unlikely but you're right, there is nowhere else she could have gone unless she can make herself invisible," Rhea agreed.

Over the weekend Ross devised a plan. Wayne would watch from the main building, Rhea would watch from the P.E. building and Ross would be inside the store. Olivia would be surrounded with absolutely nowhere to go unobserved. Just in case she managed to get on the van, Ross had his car parked near by.

He called and arranged with Ina for a hiding place. The only flaw that he could see in his plan was the fact the he may have tipped his hand when he had quizzed Olivia. She might become suspicious and outsmart them and simply go to class. On the other hand she hadn't altered her schedule after Ross had talked to her. He was confident his plan would work.

Olivia arrived at the store right on schedule. The bread van arrived right on schedule. While the deliveryman was placing his order on the rack, Olivia bought a pack of gum. She waited until the delivery man was back in his truck, then walked out the door and turned and walked with it as it began to move. Both the van and Olivia moved out of sight at the same time. "Clever," Ross thought. "No one from inside the store could see her jump on." Quickly Ross came out of hiding and wound his way around the few students and rushed out the door. Olivia was nowhere in sight and the van was just starting up again after having stopped at the stop sign just a few yards from the store.

Ross ran over and jumped in his car and followed the van around the corner and up the street. He pulled up along side and honked, got the driver's attention, motioned him to pull over, then pulled back behind him to make sure no one got out undetected.

"Hi, my name is Ross Babco. I teach at the high school back down the street." Ross introduced himself as he stood at the steps that led into the van, it being one that had a door opposite the driver's side which was often left open in good weather.

"Hi."

"We have a student that skips class, seems to disappear into thin air. We had people all around today and we are sure that the escape route from the store leads into your van."

"I believe you are mistaken Mr. Babco," the driver protested sincerely.

"May I have a look, just the same?"

The man hesitated.

"Just as a favor? The police aren't involved and you won't get into any trouble whatsoever. I'd just like to know if I'm right."

"Go ahead," the man invited with a sweep of his hand.

Ross entered the van and moved toward the back. It was a simple delivery van with wire shelves for light flour products and with absolutely no place for anyone to hide. Olivia wasn't there!

The delivery man laughed at the mystified look on Ross' face as he returned to the front.

"Crafty little devil I'd say."

"She is even craftier than I thought," Ross admitted, shaking his head.

"A girl, no less!"

Ross left quickly, humiliated by the derisive tone of the delivery man's chuckle.

TEN

Thinking that Olivia would take the shortest route uptown, Ross continued the way he was going. He cruised past the mall and the fast food places with no success. He stopped and entered a phone booth thinking that possibly Olivia had simply walked around the van and gone to class.

"Rhea? Ross here. No. I didn't see where she went. How about on your end? No she wasn't in the van. I don't have the slightest. Wait! There she is!"

It was a stroke of luck that Ross was standing hidden in the phone booth. Olivia was striding purposefully up the street toward him, not a half a block away. Immediately his mind began to race trying to decide the best way to approach her. Her turning into a building abruptly presented him with a different set of circumstances to deal with. He waited for a brief time, and then walked down to where she had disappeared.

Fuzzy's Lounge wasn't a big place but jammed inside in a hodgepodge, sprawling fashion was a bar, kitchen, dining area, a few pool tables, and a small dance floor.

He sat at the bar in a more shadowy spot. Leaning forward just a little he could look past a partition to where Olivia stood with three young men around one of the pool tables. He recognized them as former students at the high school, having graduated two or three years before. Olivia was keeping some very rough company.

"What'll ya have?" the man behind the bar asked in a generic friendly tone. He was stocky with short, very curly red hair and beard. Ross assumed he was talking to Fuzzy himself.

"Seven-Up," Ross ordered.

"Straight and on the rocks?"

Ross looked for but found sarcasm in neither voice nor expression.

"Please."

He turned his attention to the game as he nursed his drink. The boys were good players, but when it was Olivia's turn, she moved around the table with easy confidence, gesturing and speaking briefly, calling her shots which were beautifully executed. At the end of the game, Ross saw money change hands and disappear into Olivia's pocket.

"She usually win?" he asked Fuzzy.

"More often than not."

"I would say that she is good enough to beat those boys every time."

Fuzzy grinned as a knowing look passed between them.

"She must come in to play quite often," Ross observed.

"Some," Fuzzy admitted.

"Every Monday, Wednesday, and Friday," Ross stated.

A veil passed down over Fuzzy's face, leaving it completely unreadable. Ross knew he had hit the mark.

"It's not illegal for her to be in here," Fuzzy pointed out.

"But it may be illegal for her not to be in school."

"That's not my affair," Fuzzy denied all responsibility.

"No, I guess not," Ross agreed.

"They don't have truant officers anymore do they? Are you with social services?"

"No, I'm her teacher for a couple of classes History and Special Ed."

"Special Ed.? Olivia? Isn't that the same as the old remedial classes?" Fuzzy's face was a study in disbelief.

"Not exactly, sometimes we have gifted students in our class. Olivia is in there because no one could figure out what else to do with her."

Ross leaned forward to check on Olivia. She hadn't noticed him yet. The light above the table must have made it harder to see into the other areas of the room.

As she walked past one of the boys, he reached out and patted her affectionately on the fanny. Her response was immediate and automatic and very effective. With a slight twist of her body

82

and a flick of her wrists she brought the cue stick sharply down across his knuckles.

"Damn! You're a vicious bitch!" His damaged fingers were hidden in his armpit as he tried to keep from showing how badly they hurt.

Olivia proceeded to walk calmly around the table, pausing here and there to bang each and every ball violently into a pocket.

"Idiot!" one of the boys criticized. "You know she can do that when she gets mad." Again money exchanged hands.

The pool cues were put away, and the light above the table turned off. It wasn't until the four young people were near the bar that Olivia saw Ross.

"Oh, hi, Mr. Babco," Her hesitation had been ever so slight, and her greeting was as normal as if she met Ross everyday at the bar.

"Hi, buy you a drink?" Ross offered.

"Sure." Olivia sat down on the stool next to him.

"What'll it be?" Fuzzy asked.

"Gimme a beer."

"Olivia! Don't do that!" Fuzzy turned an anxious face toward Ross. "I don't sell her beer. Honest." He glared at Olivia.

"Just having a little fun, give me the usual."

Fuzzy set a frosted bottle of Squirt in front of her.

"I need to get back to class." Ross checked his watch. "Can I give you a ride?"

"I guess."

Ross paid and they left.

"You must really enjoy pool to go through all that effort to get away," Ross told her once they were in the car. Although her expression changed ever so slightly, she managed to convey that she thought this sheer lunacy.

"Of course, there are the young men."

Another slight shift of expression let Ross know that she held them in great contempt.

"Or perhaps it's just the money," Ross probed. "How much did you make?

"Twenty-five bucks."

"How does that work?"

"Each player pays five bucks to play. The winner picks up the pot. Five bucks from each of the three makes fifteen bucks a game for each of the two games I won. Thirty bucks total. I lost one game and my five bucks. Five from thirty is twenty-five."

"What would your mother say if she knew you were doing this?"

"I give my weaving money to help the family. I don't think it is wrong to have a little extra for my own wants and needs," Olivia defended.

"I meant if she knew you were hustling the customers at the pool hall."

"Oh. I don't know." This was said with total indifference.

"Now that I have discovered where you go and what you do, it wouldn't change your situation any if you told me how you managed to get out of the bread van without my seeing you."

For a brief second she didn't comprehend, and then she burst out laughing. Her laugh degenerated into a case of the giggles. Her eyes were bright and shiny with mischief.

For the first time, Ross realized that despite her tough exterior, her desires were those of any teenage girl. She enjoyed her skill on the pool table, the attention of the young men, the money she won, but most of all she needed the fun and excitement of matching wits with those in authority over her in an otherwise dull and unchallenging environment.

Ross could easily see her laughing and joking with her younger brothers and sisters in the relaxed atmosphere of her home. She was willing to sacrifice for those she loved. And yet she was alone among her peers at school. Ross wondered at the experiences she must have had to form her in her present image.

She was a beautiful person in mind, face, and form. Oh, how he wished that he could have raised a daughter like her. A lump arose in his throat, and he turned his head to keep her from seeing the tears that formed in his eyes.

"I was never in the van," she giggled.

"But I came out of the store not ten seconds after you did, and you were gone."

"I know."

"Did you know about Wayne watching from the high school?"

"Yep."

"And Rhea too?"

"Yes, I come out of the store and walk alongside of the van. North of the store is a little space of only a few feet, and then right on the corner is a little house. The van travels just a few yards then it has to stop for the stop sign. The driver doesn't even take it out of first gear nor does he pull away from the curb. I can't be seen from across the street. A few steps put me out of sight from inside the store. There is a blind spot for the driver just behind his window and just out from his mirror. He can't see me either. When he pauses for the stop sign, I have about three or four seconds to turn and run east up the sidewalk for about fifteen to twenty yards to put me behind the little house where no one can see me from the street that the school is on."

"So simple," Ross marveled.

"I suppose that you will have to turn me in," Olivia sighed.

"I suppose I should," Ross agreed . . . . . "but, I guess I won't."

ELEVEN

Sitting in faculty meeting that was held every Monday morning before school, Ross waited patiently for the business of the day to wind down before he spoke.

"Wayne, who is responsible for choosing the text books we use here in the district?"

"The principal of each school."

"Do you read them?"

"I used to, years ago, but I found that it made very little difference. You see, the Federal Government publishes a list of the books that we may choose from. Every publishing company has learned what the government wants. Accordingly, all the books are basically the same in content. We now have a committee that does that for us."

"And what does the committee look for?"

"Books with the best format and illustrations."

"I think you better start reading again. History is being changed."

"Changed? What do you mean?"

"For example, our modern text states that George Washington was almost royal in his attitude and even insinuates that he lived extravagantly while he was president. The truth of the matter is that when some of the leading officers of the military came to him after the British were defeated and offered to make Washington king, he refused. He served eight years as Commander-in-Chief of the army and then eight years as president, all without pay. He received only his living expenses."

"Can you substantiate what you are saying?"

"All the old history books contain this information."

"What do you consider old?"

"Those written over fifty years ago."

"Well, there is nothing I could do about it if I did read every book. If we rejected the books on the list, we would lose our federal funding," Wayne pointed out.

"Wouldn't it be better to lose the money rather than teach our children that which isn't true?" Ross countered.

"Without that money we couldn't afford all the computers we have, not to mention the VCRs, and all the other teaching aids. Our children would fall behind the rest of the world. How could they compete in today's world?" Robert stated his opinion.

"All of us would have to take a cut in pay," Rhea pointed out.

"The state would have to have their say. I don't think they would permit it," Ida added her argument.

"There is the school lunch program that we need to consider. The parents would be up in arms if we lost that," added a teacher.

"We might lose our jobs," another looked meaningfully at Ross.   There was a murmur of assent.

"Julia, we haven't heard from you. What do you think?" Wayne asked. Everyone fell silent, not wanting to miss Julia's statement.

"Well, I think that, uh," Julia faltered, but then she got her thoughts organized and plunged ahead. "I've read about George Washington's regal manner.   I understood it to mean that he had a certain dignity about him that was noticeable by all who knew him. All this hullabaloo is nothing more than a difference of opinion over the intent of one or two historians. By and large, today's history only varies in the modern use of the English language as opposed to how it was used in the eighteenth century."

"Very good." . . . . "That's right." . . . "Exactly," were the phrases that Ross heard in response to his wife.

"We appreciate the fact that Ross is concerned about what our kids are learning, as we all are, and I think this little discussion has been good for us. We don't want to get complacent. All should make the effort to understand just how things stand," Wayne summarized. "Now then, the last item on the agenda. Ross, did you manage to discover where Olivia goes, and how she has managed to evade us for all these months?"

"Yes, I did," Ross answered, but offered no explanation.

"Go ahead and report," the principal prodded.

"Wayne, she doesn't want to be in class at that particular time. We could stop her from escaping as she now does it, but she would simply think of something else. I think we would be ahead to let things be."

"I see. Would you mind, just to satisfy our curiosity, telling us how she gets out of the store undetected?"

"She walks out the front door." Ross smiled at Wayne's expression.

"Then into the bread van is the only place she could go," Wayne smiled in triumph. "You yourself made that same deduction."

Ross shrugged his shoulders.

Man and wife fell in beside each other as they left the conference room and walked down the hallway toward their respective classrooms at the far end as they had done for countless other times through the years. But missing was the companionable silence or the friendly discussion that had characterized their relationship. Somehow everything felt different although to the eye nothing had changed.

Hair styles and fashions of the kids changed constantly, but the kids themselves were essentially the same. Teachers were pleasant and helpful people, for the most part sincere in wanting to help and to get along, loyal to the school, accepting of the directions handed down from their superiors. The atmosphere of academia had seduced Ross until he had come to thrive on the excitement of the young and the feeling that he had become an important part in forming the minds and attitudes of the rising generation.

He believed when he read Daniel Oman saying that teaching was the noblest profession. Then why did he feel like an alien walking these hallowed halls? He sighed heavily.

"You're being stupid," his wife said suddenly as if he had been visiting with her. "If you're not careful you may jeopardize your contract for next year."

"Julia, dear, my contract for next year was lost months ago," he said impatiently, but then realized that he hadn't confided in her the reasons for his being reinstated.

She stared at him hard for a minute.

"If that is the case that would explain a lot."

"Explain what?"

"Your resentment and bitterness. Why else would you be so rebellious? Really, Ross, it is very unbecoming of you to act this way."

"And embarrassing for you, no doubt," Ross recognized the sarcasm in his own voice.

Julia's face was closed and cold as she turned into her classroom without answering.

Sitting in his car at mid-block in position to watch the little drama unfold, Ross was quickly rewarded. The bread truck nosed up to the stop sign with Olivia walking alongside. Suddenly she sprinted the few yards up the street, then dropped back to a walk and casually stepped behind a large tree.

Quickly, the bread truck moved up the street with the driver going through the gears as he hurried on his way. Another vehicle careened around the corner in pursuit and moved up alongside the truck. Ross could see Wayne motioning for the truck to pull over. Watching the pantomime, Ross smiled to see the Principal duplicate his actions of the previous Friday. Only the greatly increased amusement on the face of the truck driver prevented the scene from being an exact reproduction.

More pressure was brought upon Ross at the next faculty meeting concerning Olivia's continued sluffing.

"You know, Ross, you aren't doing the girl a favor by remaining silent," Rhea stated. "If she doesn't get credit in my class she will not graduate. It has gotten to the point that I will have to flunk her no matter what, if she doesn't make a big effort to attend and to do some make-up work. I'd be willing to stay after school and let her go through the program."

"I'll talk to her," Ross promised. He made good on his promise that very afternoon. He signaled for Olivia to come to his desk as the students began filing out.

"Olivia, Rhea has just informed me that in order to graduate, you must get a grade in her class. With each passing year it becomes more important than ever to get your schooling in order to make a good living. I want you to consider and weigh the effort made for two or three weeks against a whole lifetime of working at low paying, menial jobs. I'm sure you can see the wisdom of what I am saying."

Olivia nodded her head in agreement.

"Good," Ross felt relieved that things were going so well, "I'm sure you'll never regret your decision."

"No, I don't think I will," Olivia agreed once more, but her expression was at variance with her mild words.

"You are going to start attending again?" Ross was suddenly uneasy.

"No."

Students began entering for Ross' next class.

"Look, I know how important it is for you to have a little money for your own and to have a little excitement, but to throw away a whole future for a few days of pleasure is foolish. I can't let you do that. Promise me you'll go back."

With a slight shake of the head, Olivia started for the door, her face a study in defiance.

Ross followed after her out the door and seized her by the arm, stopping her and pulling her out of the mainstream of students flowing past in the hall.

"You are way ahead in my class. I could in all good conscience give you a good grade if you did nothing more. If you will promise me that you will go to P.E., I will excuse you from my class. It's later in the day. There should be more people at Fuzzy's, greater possibility to make more money, have more fun."

Ross, looking intently into her face saw that she never even considered the offer. The second bell rang. The last of the stragglers cleared from the hall leaving them alone.

"That's not it, is it?"

Olivia looked away,

"Can you tell me what's wrong?"

Olivia stood silent, looking into the distance waiting for him to release her.

He sighed in defeat and dropped his hand from her arm, thrust his hands into his pockets and stepped back. One last idea popped into his head.

"Is it Rhea?" he asked.

Olivia's eyes flickered and seemed to grow brighter. Still she didn't speak, but neither did she attempt to leave even though Ross had given her space.   Several long moments passed before he realized that she was angry.

"Do you want to tell me about it?"

She shook her head but still made no attempt to leave.

"I understand that she is quite well liked by her students."

"Almost everybody."

"But not all?"

"There are one or two that are her special ... pets."

"She plays favorites.   Does that make a difference to you?"

"There are one or two who hate her guts."

"For showing partiality?"

Olivia's head bowed and turned to the side, hiding her face behind a veil of long dark hair. Her voice came so low and muffled that Ross could barely hear her.

"She wants me to come in alone after school to do make up work or go over to her house when her husband is gone and she is always offering me a ride home."

"Olivia, sometimes a rumor can get started that will color a person's judgment, cause them to think they see that which really isn't there. I've seen this happen before.   An innocent person's career ruined. I'd hate to see that happen to Rhea."

"There is no rumor. She is very careful, but one time she asked me to put away the volleyball net while she went into her office with one of her pets.   Later when she came out she was still buttoning her blouse. She looked me right in the eyes and smiled. When she walks by the shower room and looks in at us it makes my skin crawl."

"You feel her actions were an invitation, but you have no concrete evidence."

"No."

"You can't endure your discomfort for the thirteen days even for a diploma?"

"No," Olivia's answer came quiet, flat and final.

Ross stepped across the hall and told Julia that he would be walking home, and then hurried down to the Phys. Ed. building in hopes that he could catch Rhea before she left for the day. Luckily, all the students were gone, and Rhea sat at her desk with the office door open. Ross pushed the button on the doorknob in as he pulled the door closed behind him to ensure that they would not be disturbed.

"Hi," Rhea greeted cheerfully, "what brings you down from the mind building side of education to the body building side?"

"Oh, I was just passing by and thought I'd say hello. I'm sure glad we live in a smaller town."

"Why is that?"

"I read an article a short time ago about a teacher that seduced a student. The teacher was charged with statutory rape, but the defense attorney argued that it wasn't rape because being seventeen and old enough to realize what she was doing, the young lady had willingly and with full consent, engaged in sex. The state however claimed, successfully, I might add, that because the teacher was in authority over her there was implied coercion. You know, her grade or even her graduation might be in question if she didn't consent. I'm sure glad we don't have to deal with that sort of thing here," Ross shook his head to indicate his amazement at the corruption of the big cities.

He had let his eyes wander all over the office hardly daring to look at Rhea, but now he stole a glance. She sat calmly, her attractive face at peace. Although of a more stocky build, she was in excellent shape and sat squarely in her chair. Dark, short hair, dark eyes and square white teeth made a very feminine and pretty picture. Even the dark, thin, downy mustache did not detract. Ross felt relieved to see her react normally to this story. He had very briefly considered confronting her openly, but was glad that he had controlled his impulse. He even felt ashamed of his unkind thoughts.

"They convicted him, you say?" Rhea asked.

"Yes, they convicted her," Ross raised his eyes and looked directly and steadily into the eyes of one suddenly very frightened woman, "sent her to prison, ruined her career. Her husband left her."

In shock, Ross walked back toward the high school. He was certain now that Olivia had told the truth. He had been just as certain that she had been mistaken when he had gone to visit Rhea. In retrospect, he realized that Rhea would think that he had known and that he had threatened her, but in truth he had added the last part of the story only when she had acted so normal up to that point.

Seeing the situation from Olivia's point of view changed things immensely. He was sure that Rhea had considered Olivia to be the perfect target; lonely, seemingly having a dislike for boys, no dates, smoking cigars, and other symptoms of rebellion. Not to mention her comeliness. Ross found himself in a quandary. He didn't want Olivia to go back to Rhea's class at all, not even the two days a week. He felt the need to intervene somehow, but what could he do? He had no proof. Wayne should know, but Ross didn't feel that he could approach him without more proof than an expression on Rhea's face. At that moment he understood the leap of faith it had required for Olivia to have confided in him. He didn't have that much faith in the principal.

Ross came out of his reverie to find himself standing motionless on the sidewalk in front of the school, looking at the window to the principal's office.

"Wayne, what is the district's hiring policy concerning homosexuals and lesbians?"

"We don't have one."

"Has the district ever hired one?"

"I don't know. That is not one of the questions on the application nor is it asked in a personal interview."

"Why not?"

"The public schools are just that, a public institution. We, by law, are not to violate anyone's civil rights by discriminating against any minority."

"So the district is very careful to not know, to avoid trouble?"

Wayne shrugged. "Why the sudden interest, Ross?"

"I've been following the case where the woman teacher seduced her female student. I was just wondering what the district would do here in a case like that."

"Nothing, I'd guess. It would be handled by the law enforcement, just like in that case."

TWELVE

"Hello, may I speak with Olivia please." Ross had stopped at a phone booth on his way home.

"Olivia! Telephone!" Ross could hear a little girl's voice yelling almost before she was away from the mouthpiece.

"Hello?"

"Ross Babco. I think that if you were to go to Rhea and ask to be excused from her class for the rest of the year that she would grant permission."

"Would I get a grade, do you think?"

Apparently, Olivia still hoped that two days a week would be enough to get at least a D and still graduate.

"I don't know, but there are some things that are more important than getting a formal education." Suddenly it occurred to him that he was giving Olivia advice completely contrary to his advice from only a few hours prior.

"Okay, I'll try it," Olivia agreed dubiously. "Thank you for calling."

Dinner was ready and on the table when Ross walked through the door. Julia was also ready with her accusing eyes. More and more, Ross was delayed for one reason or another and was neglecting to do his part preparing the food.

"Very good," he complimented, spooning in his chowder.

Julia ignored him.

"Sorry I was late getting home. Something very important came up," Ross tried apologizing.

"I'm sure it did," her voice said. Her tone said, "Humbug."

Making an effort to do more than his share with the clean up, Ross attempted to lead the discussion around to Olivia's dilemma, but Julia was in a rush to get to her T.V. program and paid little attention. Ross never found an opening. On the hour, Julia hurried in to switch on the set.

Ross finished the odds and ends, and then went to join her.

Smiling now at the comedy, her mood had softened. The warmth of her body as he sat next to her penetrated his and softened his own mood. Her relaxed, happy face reminded him of the many years they had spent together, of the many evenings sitting just like this and visiting comfortably.

He commented on the program, she answered absently.

"We should do more things together like we used to," Ross commented.

"That would be nice."

Ross waited for a commercial, hoping to get her full attention.

"Remember how we used to come home from school and share the experiences of the day?"

"I'm not the one who has changed," Julia answered.

"What do you mean?"

"You are the one that locks himself up in the study every evening."

"I don't either. I may close the door so it will be quiet enough to read, but I don't lock the door. Besides I've tried to share with you the things that I have learned."

"You act like you're the only one that knows anything. You read old books, but you don't even watch the news any more. How do you expect to know what's going on right now in our modern age?"

"All you'll ever hear of the news are the headlines. Most of the important underlying facts are left out. I've come to know that if you hear nothing more than the headlines you get a very distorted view," Ross argued intently, but the commercial was over and Julia's eyes had shifted back to the T.V. and she missed his last point.

Even an argument couldn't produce enough adrenalin to withstand the numbing, hypnotic lure of the big screen.

Fifteen more minutes of crude drivel that passed as comedy was all Ross could stomach. At the next commercial, Ross patted Julia's hand then arose with a sigh and went to the study.

During his free period, Ross and Wayne stood talking in the doorway to the principal's office while they watched Robert striding up the hall. Without waiting for a break in the conversation, Robert interrupted the moment he arrived.

"Wayne, you've got a student out on the football field sun tanning."

"I know. She has my permission."

"She does?" Robert said in surprise.

"She does," Wayne reaffirmed, but he offered no explanation. Realizing that he wasn't going to get any more information, Robert walked away shaking his head.

"Ya know, Ross, that was one of the more singular experiences in my career when Olivia came in with a note from Rhea excusing her from class. She laid it on my desk without explanation and just stood there waiting. I've been a principal in three different schools, covering a span of twenty-two years, and I thought that I'd heard every reason and excuse in the world by students trying to get out of class. Without fail, they try to bargain, offering to do extra work, extra reports, or do some service to a teacher, or to the school. When I asked her what she planned on doing during the class time, it was no idle conversation. I felt totally prepared. She looked me straight in the eye and said, 'Play pool and sun tan.' She caught me completely off guard. Not in all my years has someone told me so honestly what they intended on doing.

As she stood there waiting so patiently, I couldn't immediately think of an answer, so I gave her permission."

Marking the roll in his fifth period Special Ed. class, Ross was reminded that Todd hadn't been to class for three days.

"Anybody know if Todd is sick?" he asked the class.

"Oh, no," Missy chimed up helpfully, "he's dropped out."

"Dropped out?"

"Yeah, he doesn't go to school anymore. He works at Jay's Market," Missy explained.

Later in the afternoon Ross made it a point to go shopping. He finagled around until Todd, the new bag boy, helped him with his purchases out to the car.

"Thank you. Todd . . ."

"It's no use Mr. Babco. I know what you are going to say."

"Why did you wait until just before graduation?"

"It's no use. I won't ever be accepted into college. A high school diploma doesn't mean anything anymore. Everybody gets one whether you learn anything or not."

"Employers still ask how much schooling a prospective employee has received."

"Yeah, but if they look at my grades, they'll know I received social promotion."

"They will also note that you improved the last two years, and they will certainly note that you gave up just before graduating. Some employers still look at a person's character as well as academic skills."

"You once said that if a person learned to read well, he could learn anything else. Thanks to you, I finally learned to read before I quit. Now I can work and save my money and read about how to invest it. I'll be as well off as anyone."

"Will you quit two weeks before you succeed each time?"

"Mr. Babco," Todd cried in frustration, "you just don't know what it's like!"

"I was in Special Ed. when I was in high school. I understand."

Todd's surprise was very evident.

"Yeah, but that was thirty years ago. Things are different now."

"Closer to twenty," Ross corrected.

Todd shrugged, unimpressed.

Graduation day found Ross, for the second time that year, clearing his personal effects from his classroom. Students came requesting autographs for their yearbooks as they had in years past. An occasional visit from his colleagues interrupted his work from time to time. Each noted what he was doing though none commented. Although neither he nor anyone else had received word on his present status, he was sure that the rumors would fly concerning his departure.

That evening found him sitting alone in the audience at graduation exercises. Julia was involved with the presentation of the graduates.

He had chosen a back row seat to avoid mingling. Just as the Master of Ceremonies stood and the buzz of the crowd subsided, Don slid into the seat next to him.

It was a nice program as far as graduation exercises go. No better nor worse than the many he had attended over the years. He was very pleased to note that both Olivia and Todd sat on the stand in their caps and gowns with the other graduates. A feeling of satisfaction and personal achievement permeated his being as he thought back on the many hours spent working with these two struggling souls.

Last on the schedule of events was the presentation of special wards and scholarships. As each student who was receiving a scholarship was announced, he stood. By the time all had been presented the full front row consisting of the honor students was standing. In the rows behind, there was a student standing here and there.

"Well, Ross, how did you enjoy watching the class of eighty-nine being divided into classes according to their chance for learning?" Don asked.

"What do you mean?"

"Take Millie Parker for example; intelligent, pretty, popular, and an honor student. Her parents are quite well to do. She received three different scholarships. All awarded by academia of the state and all applicable to the same state university, right?"

"Yes, she is an excellent student. She has worked hard, she deserves it."

"She will continue her education, get a degree, and receive a license from the state certifying that she is qualified and may legally work in her chosen field. She will earn a good salary and continue to live comfortably as she does now. Would you say her life might follow that course?"

"She has every opportunity to succeed," Ross conceded.

"Now in contrast, let's examine Olivia's prospects. She is intelligent and pretty. Brilliant actually, and I'm not saying that just because I'm her uncle."

"I know, I agree."

"Her mother is poor. She is planning to weave full time to try and improve the opportunities of her younger siblings to get an education. All her work will be taxed and will be used to help pay for Millie's education. Thus the economic distance between the girls will be perpetuated, aided by the state."

"Olivia had the same opportunity to work hard in school as did Millie," Ross argued.

"Of course, so you see that even in high school the state is setting the criteria for whoever will continue to receive aid in their attempt to succeed in this world."

"Olivia is made of good stuff. She will be alright."

"I agree. But she will do it in spite of the system. It will be a difficult thing for her to overcome. But how about the other kids that were in your Special Ed class? Did they receive scholarships? If they make the struggle to attend school, their work will be taxed, making it even harder to afford tuition and living expenses."

"Danny got a football scholarship," Ross commented.

"The university will probably provide him with a tutor if he is an asset to the team. If he plays four years without disabling injuries, the state will say he is certified to work in his chosen field. He will probably be all right. How about the rest?"

Missy's parents were wealthy. They would send her to school. She would more than likely charm some young man and get married. She would be alright. But then as Ross' eyes settled upon Todd, a depression settled upon his mind. The memory of Todd's pathetic bravado, claiming that he would, by working at his minimum wage job, save enough money to make investments that would make him rich came to mind.

He too, would be taxed to help pay for Millie's education. He who had so little, with so limited opportunity to improve, would have to help those who already had so much. Ross realized that the majority of the students in his Special Ed class were in the same boat as Todd.

"The government supplements those with low incomes to compensate, to even things out a little bit," Ross pointed out.

"Yes. You've seen what welfare does to people. Can you imagine Olivia living on welfare? Would you want her to?" Don challenged.

While the two men were visiting, the commencement exercises had been brought to a close. Don rose and walked away.

THIRTEEN

His final act as an employee of the district was to be chaperon at the dance. Watching Todd and Olivia dance together, time after time, he realized that she was his date. They were laughing and having a good time, ignoring the looks of amusement they were receiving. She stood half a head taller than Todd, who in his ungraceful shuffle, was trying to avoid running her into the other dancers in the packed hall. Olivia, in her white gown that contrasted so beautifully with her dark skin and hair, was in Ross' opinion the most striking woman on the floor.

Todd, on the other hand, looked so young and awkward, it was painful to watch. A deep melancholy settled over him as he realized he would seldom, if ever, see these young people again. Dan danced by with Missy. It was obvious that he had been drinking. Ross had received instructions to not allow anyone in that was high, but Dan wasn't being rowdy. Ross decided to ignore him.

The conversation with Don kept returning, causing his dark mood to deepen, even as the party got livelier. In an effort to shake off his depression, he asked Millie to serve at the punch bowl while he danced with Julia. He had chosen to dance to music with the right rhythm to allow him to take Julia in his arms. After years of attending the high school dances, Ross and Julia had learned to move gracefully together as one. He held her close and tenderly without speaking. The following dance was also conducive to a more romantic atmosphere.

"One more, Dear?" Ross held out his arms.

"We can't leave Millie at the punch bowl all night," Julia declined.

Ross slumped back into his chair near the door, feeling quite morose. The evening dragged on and on. "How did people sustain such exuberant good spirits for so long?" Ross wondered.

Todd approached him and held out a small, elongated package tied with a narrow blue ribbon.

"It's from Olivia," Todd waited indicating that Ross was to open it immediately.

He pulled the ribbon and unrolled the wrapper revealing a long ultra-slim cigar. He looked his question at Todd.

"There is a date on it," Todd answered.

Ross rolled the cigar in his fingers.

"March 12th," he dutifully read.

"That is the last cigar of the last box she bought. March 12th is the day she didn't smoke it."

"She's quit?"

"She wanted you to know," Todd grinned.

"Thanks Todd."

From across the hall Ross kept his eyes on Olivia as she stood near the punch bowl talking and laughing. He was pleased with the change of attitude that had slowly worked its way into her life. Although she was still very private in her thoughts, she had begun to let her personality show through more. Ross was sure that her self-image had improved considerably. Her mood swings were less pronounced.

As Todd approached her, she discreetly glanced in Ross' direction to see if Todd had done her bidding. Casually, Ross raised his closed hand with thumb extended upward. She flashed him a smile and a thumb in reply.

For the third year in a row, Tommy, Julia's nephew, the son of her sister came to spend the summer. The ginger color of his hair and his slight angular build made him look more like his aunt than his mother. Needless to say, he was Julia's favorite. She had volunteered to help him with his difficulties in school, but Ross figured that for three months Julia could enjoy having the child she had wanted, but by September each year Julia was ready for him to go home.

Tommy, just nine years old, but mentally very active was, because of considerable practice, very effective at manipulating his aunt and receiving anything that his little heart could desire, within the outer boundaries of reason.

Tommy had quickly allied himself with Julia, for he knew that Ross would not countermand decisions made by his wife, even though he often disagreed. The two males got on each others nerves. To alleviate the tension somewhat, Ross found a summer job to get him out of the house for most of the day. Deciding that he needed to do something a little different, he accepted a job at a feed lot, thirty miles west of town, owned by a long time acquaintance.

His job consisted of filling a feed truck with a feed mix from what was referred to as the mill. The mill was made up of huge granaries, a machine used to grind forage such as alfalfa and straw, tanks of molasses and alcohol and a boiler used to moisten the grain. The grain then passed through a roller to smash it flat to enable the cattle to get more of the nutrients out of it. The rolled flakes then were sucked up a sixty foot shaft to be dumped back down into different bins. The chopped hay was also blown into big bins.

Ross drove under these bins in a truck that had big augers in the box to mix the hay and grain. This truck box also contained a scale. By pushing an electrical button stationed on a post near the passageway beneath the bins Ross could fill the truck with the right weight ratios. He then pulled ahead a few feet to another station where he pushed other buttons to start the pumps that ran the right amounts of molasses and alcohol.

The rations varied according to the stage of fattening of the animals in each pen. Once Ross had learned the different rations the cattle were to receive and before it became so repetitious to him, he was quite interested.

When Tommy learned that Ross was working with real cows he wanted to go to work with him. At first he too was excited. He especially liked to watch the little door open on the side of the truck box, and the feed augured into the feed bunks as Ross drove down what was described as a feed alley. But after driving around all day to put out twenty-six loads of feed, he was exhausted and bored. He went back to helping Julia in the flower garden in the cool of the morning and to watching T.V.

On one side of each pen was a feed alley with no gates, so that the feed truck operator could drive by and feed. On the other side of each pen ran an alley for working cattle. The gates to the pens could be opened to move the animals from one pen to another, according to their size. As the animals grew they were moved from pen to pen, ever closer to the loading chute. The fattest cattle ended up next to the chute for convenient loading. Each day the cowboys rode through the corrals looking for and driving the sick up the alley to the hospital pens.

While driving by the head of the working alley one morning, Ross heard a sharp whistle. Lee, the large raw-boned cowboy in charge of the movement and doctoring of the cattle signaled for Ross. He climbed down and walked down the alley to where Lee and two or three other men were working.

"Get on that gate," Lee ordered.

Ross resented being ordered about by an over-bearing boy. Ross knew Lee was only in his mid-twenties but he was unsure of how far Lee's authority extended.

"Pardon me?" Ross thought to at least make Lee think of showing a little respect to an older man.

"When I holler 'Hold him' you swing the gate closed."

Ross stood next to the six foot tall pole fence behind a large, heavy built metal gate. On the other side of fifty animals was another closed gate, making a holding pen. Two of the men would walk through this small herd, letting them filter by where Lee could judge the animals that were fat enough to be moved to the next pen. Those too thin he waved back with his arm or sometimes with his hat. This was skillfully done, Ross had to admit. He stood motionless, feeling useless, while the other men worked.

"Hold him," came Lee's unexpected order.

The thousand pound steer was already near the gateway as Ross, with all his strength, tried to get the big gate in motion. He could see the wild-eyed steer would meet him at the fence, but was going too fast to stop. To keep from being run down Ross held back as the gate scraped along the huge animal's sides as he brushed by.

"Open the gate," Lee commanded in disgust. He walked into the cattle and deftly cut out the steer and ran him back.

"You gotta swing the damn gate closed before he gets here. Get out of the way. I'll show you." Lee took his position behind the gate. With one less man it wasn't long before a steer came charging down the alley accompanied by the shout,

"Hold him."

Lee leapt into action slamming the gate closed in the very face of the animal as it braced its legs in a skid and banged into the gate and turned away.

"See?" he quizzed Ross.

Ross nodded.

"You can't be afraid of them, or they'll get by every time." Lee turned and tromped back to his position.

"There ain't nothin' worse than an old tenderfoot," Ross heard him tell the other men with great feeling.

"Hold him!" came Lee's command a short time later.

Aggressively, Ross swung the heavy gate into the face of the onrushing animal. Too late he realized that he was too slow to stop the huge animal, but fast enough to have gotten directly into his path. Just before the gate was to click shut, the steer lowered its head and hit it with Ross directly on the other side. The gate was flung open, bashing

116

Ross across the narrow alley into the opposite fence.

He lay stunned with blood on his face as the other men rushed over. Just before he passed out he heard Lee.

"You'd think he'd have the sense to move when he could see the critter wasn't going to stop."

Ross awoke to the soft murmur of voices.

" . . . . a slight brain concussion and fourteen stitches," a nurse was explaining to a short gray-haired man in rough work clothes. They turned as Ross stirred and opened his eyes.

"Lie quiet, Mr. Babco," the nurse admonished unnecessarily.

"I'm feeling mighty bad about this, Ross," the short man spoke. "Lee knows he isn't to use the feed truck drivers. He gets to thinking his work is more important than anyone else's. My insurance will take care of everything so don't worry about the hospital bill."

"I'm not, Shelby," Ross reassured his friend.

"I hope it's not too painful," Shelby commented anxiously.

"No. I can hardly feel a thing." Ross guessed that he had been given a painkiller.

"Ross," Shelby began uncomfortably, "the doctor says you will not be able to return to work until your concussion has healed. He says it'll be two or three weeks before he'd feel good about your resuming normal activities. In the meantime, I'll have to hire someone to drive the feed truck."

"Of course," Ross agreed.

"I brought your paycheck just in case you need a little money in the near future."

Ross nodded his thanks.

"Has Julia been informed?" he asked.

"Yes, she is on her way."

After Shelby left, Ross picked up the check that had been left. It covered the monthly pay period although several days were left before it was due.

FOURTEEN

Julia arrived shortly thereafter to make all the appropriate noises of a mother hen clucking over a chick. She held the mirror up for him to see the wound beginning between his eyes and running over the bridge of his nose to end on the cheek, just below his right eye.

"They told me that it was a clean cut. It won't scar badly," Julia informed him.

Once Julia could see for herself that Ross would be all right, the conversation died down.

Discreetly she checked her watch and glanced at the darkened screen on the wall.

Ross located the remote control on the bedside stand, and the screen flickered to life then, one after another, Ross ran the programs by until he found the soap opera that Julia followed religiously.

"That the one?" he asked.

"I don't need to watch it today, for goodness sakes," Julia protested, but Ross didn't turn it off. Three minutes later Julia had been seduced and was watching, totally oblivious to anything else.

"Where's Tommy?" Ross asked once the soap was over.

"I left him in the waiting room. They wouldn't let him in to see you. I shouldn't leave him any longer." With that, Julia said her good-byes and hurried out. Ross buzzed the nurse.

His head had begun to ache terribly.

After lying around the house for two weeks getting on Julia's nerves, Ross was relieved to get back to work. His comment that Tommy ought to be down at the bowling alley or the swimming pool instead of sitting and watching those degenerative soaps had precipitated his job search.

For two weeks now, he had been pushing a wheelbarrow across scaffolding on the face of an ever-growing building. Forty feet off the ground the planks groaned, creaked, and popped as Ross struggled to keep the barrow in balance in the center of the walkway. Several times he had felt the wheelbarrow tipping. In an effort to right it, he had placed his feet wider for extra leverage, only to find he had stepped on the very edge. Fear, cold and naked, had caused his heart to leap into his throat, shutting off his breath and quickening his pulse.

"Hey, hoddy, get a move on," the brick layers would yell for more mortar.

"Hod!" came the cry that kept Ross hustling back and forth on his precarious track. Moving with complete ease along the wall, the other workers were scornful of the fear that Ross tried so hard to hide. Inevitably they would overfill the wheelbarrow at every opportunity as the crane raised the mortar to the top of the wall. Blisters on Ross' hands that had been sore and painful were turning slowly into calluses.

One of the other workers overfilled the wheelbarrow right up to the brim as Ross placed it in front of the mortar mixer.

Knowing that it only heightened their pleasure when he complained, Ross silently started back across the narrow plank. It was too heavy for him and tipped dangerously to the side. With a great effort, Ross managed to right it but not before a generous portion slopped over the side.

With pounding heart and trembling legs, Ross set it down until he could steady himself.

"I think the boss wants to see you," one of the brick layers informed him. Ross peered over the side. Sure enough the building supervisor was signaling for him to come down.

Apprehension grew as Ross walked across the lot. Even with his poor eyesight it was apparent at some distance that the boss' hard hat and white shirt were liberally doused with wet mortar.

"Explain, Babco!"

"As you must know, sir, the brick layers harass a new hoddy by filling the wheelbarrow too full," Ross excused himself.

"And you must agree, Babco, that is a cowardly, dangerous, and stupid thing to let them do it," the supervisor grated with controlled fury.

Ross was somewhat ashamed to admit the truth of the statement but his irritation was greater.

"And you must agree that for a man of your experience to walk under where a new hoddy is working is also dangerous and stupid."

Walking toward his car with his paycheck and his pink slip in his pocket, Ross was convinced that his supervisor must not agree. However he felt nothing but relief.

Dreading the time when he would have to tell Julia that he had lost another job, Ross drove to the city park and sat on a bench in the shade and tossed pebbles into the pond. The warmth of the summer afternoon worked its way with him until a pleasant lassitude had seduced him into dozing. He jerked awake as he felt himself starting to tip. With a sigh, he admitted that he was bone tired. Out of shape and pushing forty Ross concluded that he had been foolish to try to do hard physical labor. He had worked in a classroom for nearly twenty years. Surely he could find a job that would made use of his skills.

Although his salary from the school district would continue until September, he felt unemployed. With the extra work he had done he would bring in more money than his wife for the summer, and yet she had changed in her attitude also. She was thinking of him as unemployed also.

It was time to find a permanent position somewhere, but on the other hand what was the hurry? Didn't he own a home with little left to pay on the mortgage? Didn't he have a savings account? Didn't he have a small investment program that would give him spending money? Didn't he have money in a retirement program?

Julia's insurance would cover her husband, and her salary would allow them to continue to live well, if not in the style they were used to.

Even his car was new and in good repair. There was no real need for him to work, and yet . . . and yet . . . what? Somehow without logical explanation, he knew that he would slowly wither mentally and emotionally. Without malice, Julia would begin to pay for this and that, slowly but surely she would have the right to decide more and more concerning financial matters.

A mental image of himself sitting on the couch in front of the T.V. unshaven, unwashed, and uncaring caused him to shudder. Out of pure perverseness, he added a beer in hand just for good measure.

With eyes still closed Ross attributed this thinking to the haziness of sleep and promptly dozed off again.

The next time Ross checked his watch it was after five. If he hustled, he would have time to run home, take a shower and get a bite to eat before he headed to the bowling alley. Once a week he was in charge of a bowling league made up of young people from ages twelve to fourteen.

Going a little too fast, Ross had to brake hard to make the turn into his driveway.

"Damned kid!" he swore. Tommy's bicycle had been left lying on the cement in front of his bay to the garage. Carefully, he pulled around it. He had better remind his nephew to move it or he might forget and back over it.

"Hon," he called to his wife, "would you fix me a sandwich while I shower? Bowling night and I'm behind schedule."

"I guess," Julia agreed absently from the couch.

"And Tommy, go move your bicycle. Its smack dab in the middle of the driveway again."

"O.K." Tommy's inflection was identical to Julia's as they both continued to stare at the T.V.

Showering so quickly that he hardly had time to get wet, Ross threw on his clothes and headed for the kitchen. Clean! Everything was so clean. No sign of a sandwich or anything else. Julia and Tommy were sitting in the exact same spot with the same vacant stare. It occurred to him that they had answered merely to minimize the disruption of the program. It was doubtful that what he had said to them had been heard as anything more than a background noise to be silenced as quickly as possible.

They were so absorbed they didn't hear him go back into the bedroom. Vaguely, they became aware of his presence. Only the simultaneous shattering of the screen and a thunderous roar got their attention. Stunned, saucer-eyed, and slack jawed they sat in the smoke-filled room with ears ringing and watched as Ross stood his shotgun in the corner and calmly walked out the door.

The thump and the sound of metal grinding on cement started immediately as Ross backed out of the garage. Sure enough, he had forgotten the bicycle. With fresh irritation, he tromped on the gas pedal. Bouncing violently as it hit the gutter at the street, the car tromped the bicycle into a flattened heap. Ross ran over it with front tires, then shifting into drive he ran over it again with both sets of tires.

Trying to keep each boy bowling in his order kept Ross from thinking about his domestic affairs, but on the way home the earlier events of the evening came crowding back into his mind to bedevil him. Feelings of self-incrimination assailed him as he realized that poor Tommy was stuck in the middle of a silent war waged between himself and his wife that even the adults didn't understand.

In his irritation, he had taken a childish delight in smashing the bicycle even though the boy had ignored him and left it behind the car. Could it be that he had subconsciously wanted to punish the inattentive boy? What blame could Ross assign? Hadn't Tommy merely followed the lead of his favorite aunt?

There wasn't even a hint of surprise when he tried the bedroom door and found it locked. Walking on down the hall Ross opened Tommy's door and looked in on the boy. The light from the open door fell upon the sleeping form. Were those tear stains on his face? Feeling more like a heel than ever, Ross continued on down the hall to the den intending to sleep on the couch.

Julia had cleaned up the refuse from the shattered T.V., but the smoky smell from the shotgun and burned electrical parts was still strong in the room. The remote control dug into his ribs as he stretched out and covered up with an afghan. With a clatter, the control fell into the gaping hole in the big screen. With a grunt of satisfaction Ross settled down for the night.

FIFTEEN

Breakfast was a chilly affair despite the warm summer sunshine streaming through the kitchen window, but Ross' every request was promptly filled.

As he finished eating, he put down his napkin and pushed away from the table.

"Tommy, I would like you to ride downtown with me."

A short time later, Ross stopped the car in front of the bicycle shop, and he and Tommy walked inside.

"Take your pick," Ross told the boy.

He had to swallow hard when a few minutes later he was making out a check. The bicycle had cost more than his first car. Of course, the car had been second hand but still . . . .

Ross followed as Tommy wheeled his new possession out onto the sidewalk, his eyes shining as brightly as the bicycle's gleaming new paint.

"Do you want to ride it home?" Ross asked.

"Yeah!"

"Just remember, Tommy don't ever park it in the driveway again. Next time you will just be out of luck. Is that clear?"

"Yes, sir!"

Back home Ross sorted through the mail. Distinctive and plump, the envelope was instantly recognized as a contract from the school district. It was addressed to Julia. Some vague hope he didn't even know that he had been harboring died quietly, with only a little pain, to be mourned with a sigh and a brief melancholy sadness.

His income would now cease, he was officially unemployed, dependent on his wife.

For weeks, he looked for a job but without success. Finally in desperation he took a 'position' with the local furniture store packing and delivering furniture for minimum wage. His supervisor was the owner's eighteen year old son.

First, as Ross' funds dwindled, Julia was required to make the mortgage payment, later the light bill, and then the grocery bill. Ross maintained his car, his teeth, and his clothes, but contributed little or nothing to the family budget.

Julia no longer consulted him when she made a major purchase. All the while the trashed T.V. screen sat in the den as a monument in his eyes to Julia's vast indifference; in hers as a monument to his growing instability. She sat in front of it on the couch to read her romance novels.

Ross spent as much of his spare time as possible at the bowling alley, or when he was too physically spent after work to bowl, he sat in the city park and tossed pebbles into the pond.

Tommy returned to his family in time to

start school.   Julia's return to school shortly thereafter left Ross with the feeling that he was being left behind.   His hunger for news of his friends and past colleagues was not satisfied. Obviously, he was no longer a part of the circle, excluded even by his wife.

Doing what, at one time, he thought would never happen, he sought the opportunity to visit with Don, the only person who understood Ross' stand.

"Hello Ross," Don greeted jovially, "how have you been?"

"Fine."

"You don't sound real sure about that," Don observed.

"My yearly routine has been scrambled. I'll adjust," Ross confessed. "How's the new Special Ed. teacher doing?"

"I hear the school district is very pleased with him," Don answered.

"I assume he is teaching the sensitivity program."

"Yes, but not the blatant old-fashioned program they asked you to teach."

"What do you mean?"

"Thirty years ago, the program, as you were asked to teach it, was introduced into this school district. It was rejected by the teachers as well as the parents that were well enough informed to know about it in any detail. A more subtle plan was put in place.   Those that are now teachers have been through the system themselves and have come to accept the program as a normal and practical approach to teaching. The reintroduction of the primitive program was done to fulfill two purposes; first: to see if they had successfully indoctrinated the rising generation and second: to single out those individuals that might not conform in their thinking.

"So how many nonconformists are there?"

"Just one in this district."

"In this district?"

"Yes, just you. There are four or five statewide."

"Don, I don't quite buy that. Sure you've been right about a thing or two, but Wayne would never put up with such criteria for hiring teachers."

"Not if he were free to operate the school according to his own ideas, but even he is no match for tradition coupled with policy."

"You indicated this policy is statewide."

"It's nationwide actually," Don clarified.

"Because of Federal funding?"

"That's right."

"The school system of the state receives only seven percent of its budget from the Federal government. I would say that the state has much more influence on policy," Ross argued.

"And I would say that for seven percent, we were bought mighty cheaply," Don countered. "Have you decided yet who the party in power is?"

"I'm not sure that your premise is true, that the curriculum of the schools is determined by the party in power as asserted by Madison. The policies of this school at least have remained constant over the last twenty years despite the changes in administration," Ross pointed out.

"Very observant, I agree completely. Could it be that the two parties, both Democrat and Republican, are different wings of the same party or that the party in power is in reality a third and distinct party?"

"If it were a third distinct party, it would have to exercise control of the other two to maintain a constant policy," Ross reasoned.

"Again, I agree. Who is the party in power?"

"You tell me!" Ross burst out in frustration.

"Was there a prayer at graduation exercises last spring?"

"You know there wasn't."

"How about at city council meeting?"

"No, not any more."

"Why not?"

"The Supreme Court has ruled that it violates the civil rights of those who don't believe in God."

"Did you know what percentage of the students in the high school are Christians?"

"Ninety-eight percent, approximately."

"And the teachers?"

"Almost as many."

"For the first hundred years of our history, the Bible served as a textbook. Now to teach the account of the creation is illegal, but the theory of evolution is required by law."

"The reason for that is founded upon the doctrine of separation of church and state," Ross pointed out.

"The amendment guaranteeing the freedom of religion was to prohibit the government from establishing a state religion, and to keep the government from persecuting religious people, not to eliminate the influence of religion upon government."

"But by your own argument, government should be neutral in religious matters."

"Definitely, but the moment that government enters into education then they must make a decision on what is taught. To finance something without knowing how it is spent is irresponsible. This is the reason that when government, state or federal, funds the schools, they become secular instead of religious. But nothing can be taught in a vacuum or neutrally, values of some kind are taught. In reality, the account of the creation is not allowed in school because although there is evidence of the earth being organized by an intelligence, there is no absolute proof. Therefore it must be accepted on faith.

"It is because of this that it is defined in the dictionary as religion."

"The proponents of the theory of evolution likewise cite evidence to bolster their point of view, but they are forced to call it a theory because they too lack absolute proof, they too must accept it upon faith. Applying the same dictionary definition the theory of evolution must be classified as a religion. In view of the fact that education is compulsory, we have a state religion."

"I find it hard to accept the theory of evolution as being defined as a religion."

"It is only a tenet of a religion as the creation is only part of the Jewish and Christian religions."

"Of which religion is it?"

"The old Greek mythology mixed with Babylonian astrology and Roman civil law."

"Don! That is ridiculous! We are a modern scientific civilization."

"Western civilization was based upon what is called the Decalogue or the Ten Commandments. These presuppose that an intelligent being created the earth for the purpose of providing a home for humanity. Thus, mankind is the steward over the earth. Our state religion presupposes that the earth was formed by chance, and that mankind is only one more of the vast biological species created by the earth. Thus the earth is more important than man. It is even revered as 'mother earth'.

One religion says that we are responsible for our actions and will be judged accordingly. The other teaches that as biological animals, physical pleasure, creature comforts, and dominating our fellow beings are the sole purposes of life. There is no restraint other than fear of our neighbors, for at death that is the end of us."

"There is the law."

"The law has become so permissive that criminals have little fear of it. Drive by shootings, murder, rape, and the explosion of illegitimate births are all a result of the shift in religious thinking. Christianity taught the sacredness of life, the value of virtue. The new religion emphasizes material success with phrases such as 'If you're so smart, why aren't you rich?' Thomas Jefferson thought that the purpose of education was to maintain a moral and free people. The statement heard over and over today is 'The goal of education is to enable the student to obtain the degree that will assure a high paying job and a high standard of living.'"

"What is wrong with a pursuit of excellence in one's chosen field?" Ross argued.

"Nothing, but we have been seduced by the thinking that an honest man is of less value than a materially successful one regardless of the rich one's method of accumulating wealth."

"In other words we should choose the spiritual over the material," Ross summarized.

"Exactly!"

"Not everyone is cut out to be a minister or a monk."

"Ross!" Don exclaimed in frustration, "Why are you being so willingly ignorant? You lost your job because you chose the spiritual over the material!"

Stung by Don's criticism, Ross had terminated the conversation, but for days he wondered why Don had said he had chosen the spiritual over the material.

Sixteen

Shopping at the store where Todd worked as bag boy had become a habit for Ross. At first, he had gone merely out of curiosity to see how Todd was doing, but now he enjoyed the service he always received. Todd, always with an optimistic attitude, often carried his groceries out to the car.

"How have you been?" he addressed the boy.

"Real good."

"How's the savings program going?"

Todd's eyes slid away, "I had to buy a truck to get me to work," he explained.

"Transportation to work is a necessary investment," Ross agreed.

"I'm off work in just a couple of minutes. Want to go for a ride?"

"Sure. Why not? Which one is it?"

"The Ford," Todd pointed at a small, clean, nicely painted maroon pickup.

Once inside, Ross noted the immaculate carpet and upholstery.

"I did that myself," Todd's pride in owner-ship was evident. Going through the gears a little faster than necessary to show off the peppy engine, Todd headed for the open road.

"What did you pay for it?" Ross asked.

"Fourteen hundred. I think I got a good deal."

"You paint it yourself?'

"Nope."

Despite the fact that the little truck was thirteen years old, Ross had to agree. Only a little blue smoke came out the exhaust, when it was started, indicating that although the engine was beginning to wear, it would be good for a good many miles as yet.

"Runs smooth," Ross complimented. "Had any trouble with it?"

"Only a few minor things. Water pump, starter, stuff I can fix myself."

Throughout the drive, Ross had tried to remain upbeat, but once in his own car, a depression settled over him. On his pay, Todd would do little more than make payments, buy gas and maintain his pickup and himself. His parents would provide food and shelter. Even more discouraging was the realization that Ross was in the same situation. He too, would buy gas, make car payments, and maintain his car and, he too would rely on someone else for his continued food and shelter, just as he had relied on his parents as a teenager just before he left home.

With sudden insight, he knew why Julia had begun to act a little more like a parent and less like a wife.

Leaves lay thick on the ground, the stark twigs of the naked trees reached into the cold pale blue of a November sky. Ross, lying on the front room floor looking out the big picture window, felt as useless as human being could feel. Because of his poor eyesight, he had been unable to shift his eyes downward and still see through thick-lensed glasses; but was forced to bend his neck in order to crate furniture. After weeks of going home with a very tired neck each night, he had finally awakened one morning with a neck so stiff, he couldn't turn it without excruciating pain.

With the holidays in only a few short weeks, his boss had decided that he couldn't wait for Ross to recover and had hired someone to fill his place. Although he felt almost better and could move normally, it still hurt to bend his neck enough to look directly down.

Julia had suggested that he rake the leaves and eyed them each night as she returned from work.

"Surely your neck isn't so sore, you can't rake leaves for five minutes a day," Julia commented one evening.

"If you only filled one bag a day, the lawn would be cleared in less than a week," she said the next.

She had time to do it herself, but waited for him. He had a legitimate reason, he argued with himself, but in the face of Julia's complaining and goading, he doubted even when he had shooting pains when he moved too abruptly.

Lying flat on his back he was free of pain, comfortable and sleepy. He knew he should get up and prepare supper, but he had not done a thing all day and was not the least bit hungry. Time drifted by, until he knew Julia would be home before he could get anything done. He told himself he didn't give a damn and allowed himself to doze off.

"Ross? Ross!" Julia was nudging him sharply in the ribs with her toe as Ross struggled up from a deep sleep.

"What?!" he responded irritably.

"Telephone."

"Hello? Ross?" Don asked cheerfully.

"Speaking."

"You sound different. Are you alright?"

"Fine," Ross spoke sharply.

"A good friend of mine called this morning and told me that our mutual friend had suffered a heart attack and died."

"Sorry to hear that," Ross responded automatically. He didn't feel the least bit sorry.

"He was a history teacher at a small private college on the west coast."

"Interesting."

"The friend that called me is the college president. I told him about you. He appeared to be quite interested. He said that if you are interested in the position, you could call him and arrange an interview." Don then gave Ross two numbers. "He said it would be all right to call him at home."

Before Ross could thank him, Don had said goodnight and hung up.

"Who was that?" Julia poked her head back into the room.

"Don."

Julia's expression conveyed her distaste for the man as she turned away.

Less than two minutes passed as Ross, drumming his fingers on the table considered his options. The memory of the series of dead-end jobs spurred him to make the call.

Later, as he sat at dinner, he searched his mind for a diplomatic way to break the news to his wife. He knew she wouldn't be happy. When he did finally speak, he merely stated it simply.

"I have an appointment for a job interview with Prescott College on Thursday."

"Oh? That's nice. Where's Prescott College?"

"Northern California."

"That's over fifteen hundred miles away!"

"I know, but the holidays are only five weeks away. I'd be home then and again for spring break."

"And for the summer?"

"I assume so."

"You assume."

Excitement began to build as Ross packed for his trip. He would take a flight out to the coast Wednesday evening, find a motel and be rested and ready for his Thursday interview. If he should get the job, he would find a place to live, fly back home, pack his car with what he would need to get by until Christmas, and drive back out to the coast.

As he worked, he began to share his hopes and plans with Julia, but she turned away and left him to finish alone. He marveled at her total lack of curiosity.

Approaching the campus in his rented car, Ross' stomach began to churn. His enthusiasm and confidence began to desert him as he thought of the circumstances surrounding his pending interview. From the back of his mind where he had carefully hidden it, the thought that friends of Don's operating a private school were likely to have the same view of life as Don did. Would Ross, who had been thoroughly indoctrinated in the public schools, be acceptable to them?

The pain in his stomach was ample evidence of how badly he wanted a teaching job. A mental image of his helpless body plunging to its death into a crevasse between the land mass of public schools and the island of private ones agitated his mind.

The small size of the campus was a disappointment but the setting was so beautiful, it made his heart ache. Nestled in the trees at the foot of the snow capped Sierra Nevada Mountains, far from the sea coast, the old, well-kept buildings and grounds emitted an aura of friendliness and welcome.

The students themselves were an extension of the mood of the place. Although they were laughing, talking, flirting, and generally engaging in activities common to all young people, they were more clean cut, less ... cynical? Less... disrespectful? Less ... less ... what? Ross couldn't quite put his finger on the difference.

He walked slowly through the halls to get a feel for the place. With only a few students wandering about between classes, it was quiet and peaceful, but not in the least lifeless.

Having asked a young couple, he was directed to the main office. He was early, but didn't mind waiting. He checked his inside pocket to ensure that his resume' was there. It was. He straightened his tie, glanced down at his polished shoes.

"Mr. Austin will be right with you," the receptionist in the outer office assured him.

Ross realized that he had been fidgeting nervously. Ross watched her work. She seemed to be busy, moving from one thing to another in an unhurried, but continuous motion, not wasting a bit of energy in between. There was grey in her dishwater blonde hair, lines on her face. It was a nice face. Feeling his eyes on her, she glanced up and smiled. Ross smiled mechanically and turned his eyes away. Time began to drag.

SEVENTEEN

As Ross was being ushered into the office, he glanced at his watch. He had been waiting only five minutes past his appointment. His host also glanced at his watch.

"Sorry to keep you waiting, Mr. Babco," he apologized. Of medium height and build, with wispy white hair, and kindly blue-grey eyes, Mr. Austin would be more apt to be described as grandpa than college president. Ross guessed his age to be no less than seventy.

The grandfatherly image was quickly dispelled as Austin began the interview. Businesslike and full of energy, he wasted little time in greeting, but was not unfriendly.

"I understand that you are a history teacher, more precisely, an American History teacher."

"Yes, I've taught for eighteen years on the high school level." As Ross spoke, he reached into his pocket, withdrew his resume and handed it to Austin.

Thumbing quickly through the pages, with eyes flicking back and forth rapidly, Austin finished in ninety seconds and laid it aside. Ross' heart sank as he realized that Austin had shown no interest at all.

"Tell me, Mr. Babco, are you a Christian?"

"Yes, Sir."

"Why?"

Having never been asked this question, Ross was totally unprepared to answer.

"I suppose," Ross began after an uncomfortable silence, "I'm a Christian because my parents raised me that way." His answer sounded wishy-washy even to his own ears, but it was the truth.

"Would you say that your personal standards parallel Christian principles?"

"I would."

"Do you attend church?"

"No."

"Mr. Babco, this is considered a Christian college. The parents that send their children here, and the students that choose to come here on their own, expect to receive an education based on the historical background of this nation. History taught at this school is not a litany of dates, events, and places, but teaches political, economic, and religious theory. We acknowledge the part Christianity played in founding this country and believe that this very Christian background is the basis for the political and economic success we have enjoyed.

"Political extremes are taught only to demonstrate the negative effect they have upon the progress and happiness of the people."

"What are considered political extremes?" Ross asked.

"Socialism, communism, welfareism and statism. We don't think much of democracy either. We don't teach what is referred to as revised history. We rely on historians that were present when the events took place or at least interviewed the participants shortly thereafter. We believe the statement that 'Those that fail to learn from history are destined to repeat it for themselves.'"

Austin paused for effect. "Professor of history is considered a very important position at this school."

"Yes, Sir," Ross said to show he understood.

"I understand that you lost your position with your high school because you refused to teach revised history. Is that true?"

"No, Sir. Because I refused to teach the sensitivity program," Ross corrected.

"I see. At least your instincts are good."

"During the past year, I have researched my history and found that what was based on the works of our Founding Fathers has been changed to support the ideas that are now currently popular."

"Mr. Babco, I think you understand in a general sense what we will require. Do you honestly feel that you can teach it with conviction and enthusiasm?"

Ross understood that this was the crucial question of the interview. Everything previous had been to confirm or disprove the information that Austin had received from Don. Thank goodness, he had answered each question truthfully. The question put to him forced him to search his own mind for the answer. Various thoughts flashed through his mind as he met the steady gaze of the blue-grey eyes across the desk.

He wanted a teaching job badly. He had known that before, but now he found he wanted this job. The eyes were patient, but sharp and penetrating. Deception was out of the question. Intense study would be necessary to keep ahead of the class and to present the material properly in the high standard that would be expected. But could he commit totally to the new ideas? With a slight shock, he realized that slowly over the past year, his own examination of the public school system had been leading him to the same conclusion that had been so succinctly been expressed to him here in this office.

"I do."

For the first time, Austin looked pleased.

"Your salary will be less than what you are accustomed to. We have been in court with the Federal Government. They contend that although we as a school did not accept Federal Aid some of our students did. Indirectly, they argued the school benefited from a government program. Therefore, they had the right to dictate certain aspects of our policy and curriculum. Rather than allow the government to turn our school into another of their propaganda mills, we do not allow our students to accept federal loans, grants, or scholarships."

"They won the court case?" Ross asked.

"It is their court. We have launched a program to solicit funds which has been very successful up to this point, but many of our donors are not rich and will be one-time donors, although they feel that we are doing what is right and that we have an excellent program. Others feel that one good-sized donation will fulfill their responsibility. There are many that would like to make donations and don't have the funds, but they do send their kids here. A few are steady contributors, but the bottom line is that to continue to operate and to offer scholarships to compete for the good students, we must economize without sacrificing quality education. Our staff must be committed to the ideas upon which this school operates." Mr. Austin at this point handed Ross a contract.

"May I take some time and study this?" Ross asked.

"Certainly."

Ross noted that Austin seemed a bit tired or was it discouragement? There was a piece of pertinent information that Ross didn't have, he was sure.

"Mr. Austin, I do want the job and I appreciate your circumstances, but I'm a bit perplexed. What do you consider a qualified applicant? I'm a high school teacher, and, quite frankly, the premise that your school is founded upon is completely new to me."

"Degrees to teach history on the college level, experience doing the same, an understanding of the importance of free education, meaning free from government mandate, not free lunch type, and well recommended."

"I'm sure you can see the discrepancies as well as I."

"You come well recommended. Don is a well trusted friend. He is very impressed with you. The other men I interviewed all seemed to be fine men, but none have demonstrated that their students are more important to them than their salary, than the school, than the administrators and the state itself. Even a mandate from the Federal Government is nothing compared to what is right. Yes, you come highly recommended."

Later that evening, Ross called Julia from his hotel room.

"Hi, Honey," he tried to sound normal, "I got the job!"

"I'm happy for you," Julia answered without inflection. "Tell me about it." She listened without comment as he enthusiastically reviewed everything that had happened.

"Our phone bill will be horrendous," she finally stopped him.

149

"One more item, there are still scholarships available here, and I'm allowed to make recommendations. I told Mr. Austin about Olivia. He said she sounded like a welcome addition to the school. I'm authorized to contact her and offer her one."

"Her grades aren't that good. Might it be that she is Don's niece?"

"I didn't mention that. I'd like to see her have the opportunity myself. Would you call her and ask her to get a copy of her transcript? Make sure her scores for the ACT and CLEP tests are included. She did so well on those. Or you could pick them up yourself. That would be even better. It could be a surprise for her."

"I'll call her and tell her what's needed."

Ross spent the next few days tying up the loose ends to facilitate his move to the coast. Once he was ready, he was anxious to leave.

"I would like time to move in and unpack before I have all that studying to start on," he explained.

"When are you planning to leave?"

"Wednesday afternoon or possibly even Tuesday morning."

"Before Thanksgiving?"

"Would you mind terribly?" Ross used his most placating voice.

"Oh, no," she answered primly, "you just go have your fun. What do you want me to tell your folks?"

Julia's reminder abruptly stopped Ross' eager preparations.

"I guess I better leave on Friday."

EIGHTEEN

Over and over for the next three days, Ross checked and rechecked every detail. Twice, he went to see Olivia. Finally, it was Thanksgiving Day. Dinner smelled delicious as the two couples gathered around the heavy laden table. Ross had wanted to tell his folks about his new job in his own good time, but Julia let slip a comment here and there that required explanation. Soon the whole year long trial that Ross had endured had been laid bare.

"Son, are you sure that you have handled the situation wisely?" his father asked.

"What else could I have done?" Ross answered with a question of his own.

"I'm afraid you may have thrown out the baby with the bathwater. It doesn't take a genius to see that there are problems in the school system. There are self-serving men in all professions, but is that any reason to abandon the struggle?"

"The decision wasn't mine." Ross defended.

"It wasn't? Whose decision was it to refuse to teach the sensitivity program? Who decided to interject unauthorized history into the classroom?"

"Once I recognized the effect my teaching had upon my students, my moral conscience wouldn't allow me to continue."

"What do you think would happen to the system if every moral teacher abandoned the kids every time a textbook contained some little thing he didn't like? I'll tell you, the schools would be left with teachers without any scruples. The vast majority of the kids are taught in the public schools. Would you leave them to be taught by those without a moral conscience? Do you think that your opinion is more important than everyone else's? Wouldn't it be best to compromise just a little and take the time to look things over before making any rash decisions?"

"When I was growing up, we always went to church and, as a Sunday school teacher, you taught about the creation. Later on, before you were appointed to the State School Board, you taught biology for a number of years. How did you reconcile teaching the theory of evolution all year in school and teaching something else each Sunday?"

"For a number of years, I would announce at the start of class each year that I did not believe in the theory of evolution. I pointed out that I taught what the school district required. Each student was given the choice to decide for himself what he believed."

"So you received a year's salary for teaching the state religion that you knew was false? That smacks of priest craft," Ross concluded.

"That's preposterous! There is no state religion! Much of the evidence supporting the theory of evolution is based on careful scientific research. One should be very careful not to mix religion and science, nor church and state," the older man said emphatically.

"Mother, you have taught science for how many years now?" Ross asked.

"Thirty-eight. I started the year after you were born."

"And which slant does science put on the creation? Was the earth formed a few thousand years ago as stated in the Bible or a few million years ago as stated in our modern textbooks?"

"Science is science. Everything is based on tangible evidence. It doesn't say precisely when man walked upright and became a human as we know him today."

"God could have created men through the process of evolution. We just don't know," Julia interjected.

"I had come to the same conclusion to reconcile what I had been taught as a child and what I have been taught throughout my experience in the school system, but a more recent and careful study shows that the two are completely and diametrically opposed. And yet I believed them both at the same time. All four of us are deluded and diluted Christians, victims of a carefully planned propaganda campaign. We have compromised with a system that allows no compromise on their part. Although the vast majority of the American people are Christian, Christianity has been divorced from the public sector. Don keeps telling me that James Madison is reputed to have said that if the government financed the schools, the schools would teach the ideology of the party in power. If this holds true, the party in power is anti-Christian."

"Now son, I understand that you must feel angry and persecuted for the treatment that you have received, but don't let the bitterness color your judgment. Our school system is the best in the world, carefully built up by experience, by the democratic process into what almost all of the people want for their children. Do you really believe that your understanding surpasses that of the combined wisdom of the ages?" The senior Babco clearly included himself in this category.

"I know that if Prescott College admits only one student who has received a scholarship or grant or loan from the government, the government claims the right to impose guidelines on the entire school. I can't help but know that is the most blatant effort at thought control."

"They are only trying to help those students fit in with the mainstream of our society and culture."

"I hope they never succeed," Ross countered, remembering the clean-cut students and the peaceful atmosphere of the school.

Ross surprised even himself at the defense he had put up as the discussion degenerated into an argument. The experience at Prescott had solidified his thinking that had been developing over the past year. As the three other dinner-party members ganged up on him, he discovered just how deeply his convictions had become anchored.

Late in the afternoon his parents left, hurt and bewildered, but still concerned for his welfare. Julia avoided eye contact and went to bed early and pretended to go to sleep quickly.

Early next morning, Ross was busy transferring his baggage to the car. By eight o'clock, the vehicle was carefully packed with every available space filled. Julia had followed him out with his overnight case, the very last item. He took it from her and set it on the passenger's seat and turned back and reached out his hands for hers.

Carefully avoiding his touch, she withdrew them, folding them back against her chest. With a curious, tight-lipped expression that he had glimpsed over the past months, she seemed to be focused just beyond him.

"Ross," her voice raspy, as if she were struggling for breath, "I have instructed my lawyer to file for a divorce."

Too stunned to speak, Ross merely stood and stared.

"I think I should have the house . . . and furnishing," Julia continued with the same breathless quality. "He says . . . my lawyer says that I have grounds, and you should be smart enough to save us both unnecessary financial strain."

"Grounds?"

"Yes...desertion."

"Desertion?"

"And . . .philandering!"

"Philandering?!"

"Yes, philandering! You even had the gall to ask me to help you arrange to take the little tart with you!" Julia sputtered.

"Julia," Ross managed a forced calm, "look at me."

Her focus remained somewhere past his ear.

"Look at me!" his voice rising.

Julia's eyes darted around nervously, checking to see if anyone was around to notice. The unusual paleness of her face and the perspiration now on her upper lip, combined with the nervous twisting of her hands finally conveyed her state of mind to him. She was frightened. She had chosen the last minute in the driveway to reveal her plans in hopes that he too would not want to cause a scene where the neighbors could observe. With an unreasonable expectation, he was to accept her arrangement and drive away, leaving his memories and accomplishments of nineteen years of his life without argument, nor a backward glance.

The semi-public place was to protect her from physical violence that she feared ever since the episode with the big screen T.V. And yet he had seen this same expression before that had happened. With a clarity that shocked him to think that he hadn't fully understood it before, he realized that she had feared the changes as he had begun to examine more closely the culture that was the very fabric of their lives.

Although it was frightening for her to contemplate living without him, it was even more frightening for her to contemplate abandoning her profession, her home, her friends and her cherished way of life.

She had immersed herself in romantic fantasy both through the T.V., and when that was gone, through her romance novels, to avoid facing the reality of their situation, but finally she had been pushed into a decision.

He waited until her eyes met his.

"I'm nearly forty years old. I'm fat, bald, and blind. What lovely, eighteen year-old is going to become my mistress? I had trouble attracting the pretty eighteen year-olds when I was eighteen."

As soon as he paused, Julia looked away without comment.

"Olivia declined the scholarship. She's not going to the coast," Ross clarified for the record.

Refusing further comment, Julia merely waited. As unreasonable and unbelievable as it seemed, Ross could see no alternative, but to get in his car and drive away from all he held dear. He could think of no more arguments and Julia wasn't giving an inch. Still he hesitated.

"I'm sorry I murdered your T.V.," he blurted stupidly, not wanting her to think he harbored any hatred toward her.

He could see the tension in her that held her so rigid that she would more likely snap than bend, but the pain crept into her eyes. She remained silent, waiting.

"Would it make a difference if I stayed here?" Ross asked.

"No. You're not happy here anymore. You've become miserable to live with."

"I wish that things had worked out so you could have come with me."

Julia's chin began to tremble, and her eyes filled with tears.

"You didn't invite me!" she wailed.

Comprehension flooded his mind. From all her little comments on how much she loved her job and how important her students and friends were to her, not to mention all the references to what she was planning for the house and what she was planning for the next year in school led him to assume that she planned to stay put, no matter what, when in reality it was a campaign to get him to change his mind. Never once had Julia even hinted that she would go with him.

When young, beautiful Olivia had received the invitation to go to Prescott, but Julia received none his actions were misconstrued. Julia had come to believe that Ross had set his heart on Olivia.

"For heaven's sake, you're invited!"

"I don't want to go to California." Julia turned away and hurried back into the house.

Ross sighed and let his eyes wander up and down the street, his street for these many years. Little details he had never seen before caught his eye, familiar sights seemed strange. His house as familiar and as much a part of him as the face he saw in the mirror now seemed as alien and impersonal as a real estate ad in the newspaper. Mentally and emotionally his focus and desire had been transferred to a distant city, a different life. A deep melancholy settled over him as he turned back to his car and opening the trunk removed two of his suit cases and followed his wife back into the house and back into the bedroom. Lying absolutely still on her face on the bed with her hair down around her face hiding all expression did not conceal from Ross the fact that she was crying. He set one suitcase on the floor and the other flat on the bed and opened it up and began to put his clothes away.

"What are you doing?" Julia's question was accusatory.

"I'm putting my clothes away."

"What about your job?"

"I'll call them and tell them I can't come."

"I suppose you will blame it on me."

"I will tell them the truth as simply and plainly as I can. I think they will understand and accept that better than any other explanation."

"You are trying to make me feel guilty." Julia began sniffling again.

"You should feel guilty only if you have done something wrong."

"You think I'm selfish just because I won't give up everything and go and do what you want but I think you are selfish for asking me to. If you weren't selfish you would do what I wanted."

Ross unfolded a shirt and hung it up in the closet. The gesture was not wasted on Julia.

"You just did that to make me feel guilty, to show me you are better than me but you are mad, and don't deny it."

"I am mad. You are mad. I am selfish for wanting to run off and do what I want and you are selfish for wanting me to stay here and give up a job I want badly. I'm selfish for wanting you to give up a job you want to do and go with me. We are just alike. So what do we do?"

"Why didn't you just get in the car and drive away?" Despite Julia's frame of mind this was not meant to irritate him but was asked sincerely.

"Julia, dear, don't think for a minute that I believed you had consulted a lawyer. It was a maneuver. No lawyer would take a case on those grounds. Legal desertion is completely different than what I was about to do and infidelity; you can't cite one piece of evidence because there is none and you know it."

"You didn't answer my question?" Julia pointed out.

"I, of course, recognized that although you hadn't consulted a lawyer you had thought of it or you wouldn't have been able to say it."

Julia waited calmly although she still had tears in her eyes. He knew what she was after and he knew that she knew that he knew. He looked away.

"It should be obvious by now that I still want you to be my wife." Ross said impatiently.

She waited.

Ross hung up another shirt. She waited.

"And of course, logic follows that if I still want you for a wife it is because I'm still in love with you."

"Was that so terribly hard to say?" Julia was pleased.

It had been terribly hard to say. He was still angry and she had maneuvered him, trapped him, forced him, captured him, the battle was lost to her. Ross hung up a pair of pants and put his extra pairs of socks into the drawer. He began to ferry his shaving gear, soaps, shampoos and towels into the bathroom while Julie watched silently. Once again all the problems of the past year loomed up between them and the tension hung heavy in the air. Julia realized her victory was not complete and that even though Ross had surrendered to her he would resent it.

She faced a new dilemma. His love for her was still strong enough to hold him but every hour of his subjection would weaken it. He had made the sacrifice and now she must also, but she could not as yet face his leaving or the abandonment of her life. Foolishly she tested him further rather than seek reconciliation.

"It won't do any good for you to stay here if you continue to act the way you have in the past."

"I'll buy you a new T.V." Ross stated flatly.

"It's not just that." Julia pushed. "We have to get back to sharing our lives like we used to. We need to share the cooking of dinner like we used to and other chores and work."

"I'll do my share." Ross promised.

"It's not just that either. You hide up in the library and I sit in the den. We are like two ships passing on the sea on a dark night. We travel the same trade routes but never see each other. Do you realize that when you sit at the desk and study and I sit and watch T.V. we are back to back with only the wall between us?"

"I never thought of it."

"And do you realize that it is you that has moved? The day you walked down the hall on your present path you never came back."

"Yes, I know."

"If we are to be happy together again you must come back to me. You can't change me into something totally alien to my nature."

"No," Ross conceded mildly.

"And I don't want to argue about education or history or any of that."

"Of course not," Ross acquiesced.

"And don't just humor me!" Julia was irritated.

"I'm not just humoring you. I will live just the way you want us to. I will not discuss anything you chose not to nor will I criticize or push," Ross promised.

Julia knew that Ross would be as good as his word, he would live just the way she said she wanted to, she knew he could do it without an outward sign of rebellion or ill will and yet he was not conquered and she felt afraid.

"And you will give up the notion of teaching at some "on the fringe" institution?"

"I will not accept a position without your approval." Ross answered.

"Don't hedge. I know you. You are up to something."

"I'm merely giving you the opportunity to change your mind."

"Because you think I will? Is that it?"

"Yes. I am not making you unhappy. You love order and security, a secure and pleasant position. You hate confrontation, contention, messy situations. You have some fine Christian virtues: kindness, love, good intentions, generosity and patience. People enjoy your cheerfulness and helpfulness. You like teaching, it is who you are. It replaces the disappointment of home and family with a society of beloved friends. Is that not true?"

"Yes, it is true!"

"And you blame me for ruining it. That may be true also but it is now too late for you."

"What do you mean?"

"In my interview with Mr. Prescott he asked me if I was a Christian and when I told him I was, he asked me why. I've thought about that a lot since then and now I ask you; are you a Christian?"

"Don't be absurd. You know I am."

"Why?"

"Are you questioning my belief in Jesus?" Julia was insulted.

"No, I am going to tell you why you are going to be unhappy whether I am here or gone to California, whether we are husband and wife or if we are divorced, whether I help with dinner or I don't. Since my interview with Mr. Prescott I have taken to reading the Bible. In chapter eight of John it says ". . . and ye shall know the truth and the truth shall make you free." Contrast this to the phrase 'compulsory education'. Picture compulsory education as a huge prison wherein all roam free and study their electives but are not permitted to leave. Discipline is not permitted and student and teacher alike are subjected to the ever increasing chaos. Gun detection or metal detectors are placed at the doors and policemen roam about the halls. Compulsory education is not confined to the schoolhouse but the great prison encompasses all institutions. There is no escape for student, teacher or policeman. Chaos increases as students seek liberation through rebellion - drugs, gangs, shooting sprees and other symptoms of social unrest. There are no walls to scale, undermine or tunnel under, no bars to saw through, locks to pick or keys to steal. No physical restraint yet it is all based in the natural world - science, the laboratory, philosophy which is reason. There is no appeal to the supernatural for this is mere superstition as useless as a pizza induced dream.

For your school this is in the future but the symptoms are already beginning to appear. What agitates you is that you have seen a glimpse of a different world, a supernaturally influenced world that you still believe in, a world you cannot deny. This glimpse came through me and you seek to kill the messenger, not literally, of course, but you think the vision will disappear once the conduit is closed. But it is too late. The vision of a free and noble people will haunt you. Your innate desire to teach and help will condemn you. I need merely wait until your own nature conquers your natural man."

"You'll wait a damned long time!" Julia yelled.

"No more than a dozen years... maybe fifteen," Ross replied.

"You can't put this on me! You are not going to sit around here looking amused waiting for me to crack! I'm not going to accept the responsibility of your missed opportunities!"

"But you have demanded it," Ross told her reasonably and with that turned away and went out to the car to continue his unpacking. Julia was gone from the bedroom when he returned and he didn't see her for many hours.

The approaching dinner hour was announced by the aroma of warming left-over turkey. Ross went to the kitchen and got out the left-over salads and set the table. He chilled a bottle of carbonated apple juice. Julia appeared and took the turkey out of the oven and they sat down to dinner.

"I have thought of re-instituting grace at meal times like we did when we were first married," Ross suggested. "What do you think?"

"Fine," Julia acquiesced tiredly.

Ross said grace.

"I've always liked leftovers from Thanksgiving, especially the dressing. I like it a little bit drier." Ross said conversationally. Julia didn't reply. After dinner Ross helped clear the table and Julia loaded the dishwasher. Later Ross put the dishes away, got his book and joined Julia on the couch in the den. She glanced at his book and he glanced at hers. She noticed that he was reading a history book but didn't comment, he noticed that she was reading a romance novel and he didn't comment either. He went to bed early. She quietly slipped into bed late so as to not disturb his sleep. He stared up into the dark long after she came to bed while she lay with her back to him and watched the minutes flick by on the digital clock radio.

Julia cooked breakfast while Ross raked the leaves from the lawn. Julia began to clean the house as Ross bagged the leaves and set them out for the garbage man. He paused in his work and looked at the overcast sky through the naked, apparently dead branches of the trees. Snow was forecast and the temperature was cool but not bitter cold. He checked his watch as the van from the furniture store came around the corner down at the other end of the block. They were only a few minutes late. Once it was stopped two men got out and one opened the side door, slid a ramp out from beneath the van and wheeled a large box down the incline onto the side walk.

"Where would you like it Mr. Babco?" he asked cheerfully. "It would be more convenient to take it through the garage," Ross indicated the direction they should take. The garage door was open and Ross had moved Julia's car out of the way. With little struggle the two men managed to maneuver the tight corners and placed the box in the den. Ross asked if they might use their cart to remove the old T.V. and put it out by the bagged leaves for the garbage man which they readily agreed to. Having heard the activity Julia had come in and stood in the doorway to watch. After the men left Ross began to remove the cardboard. Julia after a moment's hesitation began to help. A few minutes later the New T.V. sat in its place dominating the room. Ross plugged it in then opened the smaller box that they had found inside and took out the remote control and handed it to Julia.

"Merry Christmas," he said with a sardonic smile.

Julia gave him a sharp look.

"It was a joke," Ross assured her.

Ross carted the dismantled box outside and stacked it beside the bagged leaves and went back inside. He was surprised to find Julia working in the spare bedroom rather than sitting before the new T.V., her abrupt movements betraying her mood. Ross retreated to the garage and puttered around at cleaning and organizing. He helped with lunch, then went down to the alley and bowled. Later in the afternoon he read and dozed and read some more. He helped with dinner, he helped with the dishes. After dinner he went to the den and finished his book. Later he found Julia sitting in the den reading her romance novel. He went to bed early. Julia slipped quietly into bed much later so as not to disturb his sleep. Ross lay on his back long there after and stared up into the darkness. Julia lay with her back to him and watched the minutes flick by on the clock radio. Ross was up early and showered. He entered the bedroom in his robe and addressed his wife.

"Would you like to go to church with me?" he asked.

"No."

Ross left early for church after fixing himself toast and juice. He walked the few short blocks in the cold fall air. He found it interesting to see who attended church and who didn't. The sermon was well prepared and thoughtful but not really inspiring. There was a spirit of peace. Ross was glad that he went even though some members of the congregation could scarcely hide their curiosity and facial expressions full of speculation at why he had decided to return to church after so long an absence. After church Ross took the long way home and sat in the park and tossed pebbles into the pond but the cold seeped into his bones and drove him home.

Sunday dinner was ready and it was very tasty. Julia had made a special effort and he complimented her on it. He helped with the cleanup, then went to the library and began to read the Bible. He left the door open. Full and warm and physically content Ross quickly succumbed and started to play rubber neck, as Julia called it. His head would begin to slowly cant to the side then he would straighten up only to have his eyes gradually close and he would begin to cant to the other side. The book would lower and plop into his lap waking himself just enough to sit up and focus his eyes once again on the page. The process began again. He read the same paragraph again and again but when he dropped the book altogether he gave it up and taking his shoes off he stretched out on the couch and took a nap.

When he awoke it was growing dark outside even though it was not late. He got up and wandered into the kitchen where he found Julia staring into the refrigerator.

"Don't worry about fixing dinner for me. Just a little snack is all I need."

"What do you want?"

"A glass of orange juice or maybe a little popcorn. If there is a good movie on T.V. we could 'spend the night at the movies'."

Julia shook her head. Ross suspected that the new T.V. had never been turned on. Past experience told him that Julia viewed the T.V. as a sin offering and if she turned it on she would be obliged to forgive him which of course she was not willing to do at this point.

"Would you like to play a game of scrabble?" Ross suggested.

"Alright," Julia conceded. "I'll fix the popcorn and you go get the game."

Ross went and got the game out of the hall closet and blew the dust off it smiling to himself. It was a good move. Julia usually won at scrabble. She won. Ross suggested another game. The popcorn was gone and the players silently and carefully considered the next move. The long minutes slowly ticked by.

"Did you call Prescott College?" Julia asked.

"No. It's a holiday weekend, remember?"

"That's right."

Many more silent minutes passed. Ross was winning by a good margin. Many more silent minutes passed and Ross' lead increased. Many more silent minutes passed and Julia sat looking down at the board while Ross waited and waited for her to make her play.

"This isn't going to work," Julia stated mournfully without looking up.

"Pardon me?" Ross responded in pretended ignorance.

"You can't treat me nice for twelve years while you wait for me to change my mind."

"Am I still waiting for you to learn to love me?"

Julia's head jerked up and her eyes were wide as she stared at him. After the shock wore off her eyes darted here and there like those of a frightened animal seeking refuge from the hunter. Her hands fluttered and her voice sputtered but finally she realized that her soul had been bare before him from the start. This knowledge came as a relief to her but the ramifications were terrible and she was frightened.

Ross stood and gathered up the popcorn bowls and washed them and put them away. He put the game away in the closet and went to bed even though it was still early. Julia, much later crept into bed silently as to not disturb his sleep. Long after she came to bed Ross lay on his back and stared up into the dark. Julia lay on her side with her back to him and watched the minutes click by on the digital radio.

The alarm clock went off early for Julia had to go to school. While she was in the shower Ross got up and started breakfast and after breakfast while Julia went to paint her face and comb out her hair Ross cleared the table and cleaned up the kitchen and started on the dishes.

"Ross?" Julia had come up directly behind him, leading him to the correct assumption that she did not want him to face her.

"Yes, dear?"

"You are not still waiting for me," she blurted out and made a beeline for the door.

"You forgot your duffle bag!" Ross had always called her huge purse her duffle bag. Julia swiveled on her heel and made the complete circle without a pause and snatched her purse off the table and fled out the door. Her faced had been flushed and she looked like she was about to cry.

After finishing the dishes Ross read the paper, and checked to see if there was any mail, then he went bowling. When he came out of the bowling alley it was snowing. The storm had been slower in coming than was forecast but it had come. He went home for lunch. The phone was ringing persistently when he walked through the door.

"Where have you been?" Julia sounded agitated.

"Bowling."

"Have you called Prescott College yet?"

"No."

Ross thought he heard relief in her sigh.

"Look, I think we need to talk things over before you do anything rash," Julia said.

"Yes, dear, I won't call today."

Ross had the table set and had just begun to prepare dinner when Julia pulled up and drove into the garage and walked briskly into the house.

"Why do you always set the table before you do anything else?" she asked.

"It puts pressure upon me to fulfill the implied promise. It makes a responsible person out of me. And you always set the table last to avoid implied promises before you are sure you can fulfill them."

"I think my way is more honest." Julia said.

Julia put her duffel bag away and returned to help with the supper. She prepared the main dish and Ross did the salad. He asked her about her day and she told a little bit about her students. When everything was on the table and they were seated he said grace. Afterward they were quiet. It was a peaceful quiet on his part but for her the tension began to build.

"Would you like dessert?" she asked when they were done with dinner.

"Nope, I'm dieting again."

Julia spooned two spoonfuls of ice cream out of the carton. Ross put the food away and Julia cleared the table and put the dishes in the dish washer. Later Ross would take them out and put them away.

"Do you have homework tonight?" Ross asked.

"No."

"Wanna watch Monday night football?"

"No."

"Wanna watch something else?"

Julia shook her head.

"Tell me about your book."

"It's just silly girl stuff."

"Kind of like a chic flick?" and Ross made a face.

Julia actually smiled.

"Ross, we have to talk."

"Yes, Dear. Shall we go into the den and make ourselves comfortable?" Ross suggested.

"No. Let's sit right here."

Ross pulled out a chair for her at the kitchen table and politely seated her.

"O.K. Dear, what would you like to talk about?" Ross asked solicitously after he had seated himself close by.

"Ross," Julia began evenly, "I don't wanna go to California!" Her voice had gone up the scale with each word and ended in a long wail trailing off and cut off as her face dropped into her hands. Ross waited patiently until she had control of herself.

"You don't have to go to California, sweetheart," Ross soothed.

"Damn you!" Julia yelled. "I hate it when you get perfect, oh, so polite and proper. You won't last twelve years; I'll kill you in twelve days!" Ross waited until her rage had subsided.

"Alright, Julia, it's time to do business. Tell me what you are going to do."

"I want to stay here and teach school just like I have always done."

"I know what you want; tell me what you are going to do."

"I am going to stay here and teach school," Julia affirmed quietly.

"And what are you going to do about you and me?"

"Why do I have to decide?"

"Let's look at my choices. Can I decide to stay here and teach school?"

"No, not now."

"Can I decide to be your husband if you decide not to be my wife?"

"No."

"Then that is why you have to decide."

"I am going to continue as your wife. What about California?"

"Do I have an option?"

"You have an option," Julia sighed unhappily.

"I am going to teach in California."

Julia began to cry again. "I'm sorry; I know I'm being a bad wife but..."

"You are not a bad wife," Ross interrupted. Julia continued to cry and Ross handed her a box of Kleenex. After a time she sighed.

"It's going to be hard."

"The Christmas holiday is only three weeks away."

"I know, but after that...spring break is a long ways away and people will think...they know we haven't been getting along..."

"Let's see what happens. Maybe in the spring we will have a better perspective. Maybe you might consider taking a teaching job in California or maybe I won't like Prescott College..."

"You'll like it," Julia interrupted mournfully.

"Do you know what you need?"

"What?"

"You need a good love affair. Think of all the wonderful gossip it would create if you never said a word but flew out to Reno every other weekend and came back tanned, rested and with a smug little smile on your face and had to wear high necked sweaters to school for a week. The more

177

observant might see a brochure of some fancy hotel peeking out of your duffle bag. You might even sport a new elegant hair-do now and again. Your lady friends by nature would conjure up 'tall, dark and handsome'; you wouldn't have to say a word. They don't need to know he's short, round and balding."

"There for a minute I thought you were serious."

"I am serious."

"I meant about having a love affair."

"I am."

"It sounds so silly."

"No sillier than those romance novels you read."

"How would you know?"

"I read one this afternoon. Do women really like that stuff?"

"Yes, they do," Julia defended.

"Why don't you write up a script and send it to me and we will act it out in Reno when we get out of school for the holidays before I come home."

"Don't be ridiculous. I couldn't do that."

"It would be easy, listen. 'Julia had just had the most delightful evening watching the most spectacular celebrity filled show and dining with the young and brilliant Professor Babco. Dinner had been served late on a small round table on their balcony overlooking the city lights. The stars twinkled in the sky and the moon was rising large and bright on the eastern horizon when Professor Babco suddenly gripped her hand from across the table (Ross suddenly seized Julia's hand) and in a low voice said 'Julia my dear, what a lovely woman you are! How am I to leave you now and return to the coast,' and Professor Babco swept the table aside and took her in his arms."

"Ross! What are you doing? You're going to break the furniture!"

"Don't be shy my love!" Ross was trying to pull her close. "Don't resist, my love. I know you are a school teacher from Middle America on your first Reno vacation far from home and romantic encounters of this kind are new to you but... you drive me wild. ERRRR!" Ross managed to encircle her in his arms and bite her on the neck.

"Ross! What's gotten into you!?" Julia struggled free, knocking over a chair and backing away down the hallway.

"'She leads me on,' cried Professor Babco. He leaped into the air and pumped his arms and legs and with growl in his throat... 'ERRRR'...he charged after her." Ross acted out his words.

Julia shrieked and ran, but Ross caught her inside the bedroom door and scooping her up he threw her onto the bed.

"ERRR!" Ross growled. He was so absolutely ridiculous that Julia began giggling.

The End

www.ingramcontent.com/pod-product-compliance
Lightning Source LLC
Chambersburg PA
CBHW030335030726
47499CB00003B/778